Anonymous

Reminiscences in the Life of a Locomotive Engineer

Anonymous

Reminiscences in the Life of a Locomotive Engineer

ISBN/EAN: 9783337415983

Printed in Europe, USA, Canada, Australia, Japan

Cover: Foto ©Raphael Reischuk / pixelio.de

More available books at **www.hansebooks.com**

REMINISCENCES

IN THE

LIFE OF A LOCOMOTIVE ENGINEER.

COLUMBUS:
FOLLETT, FOSTER AND COMPANY.
M DCCC LXI.

FOLLETT, FOSTER & CO., PRINTERS AND STEREOTYPERS, COLUMBUS, OHIO.

DEDICATION.

TO THE

RAILROAD MEN OF THE UNITED STATES,

A CLASS

WITH WHOM MY INTERESTS WERE LONG IDENTIFIED, AND WHO I EVER
FOUND GENEROUS AND BRAVE, I DEDICATE THIS
UNPRETENDING VOLUME.

THE AUTHOR.

PREFACE.

BRAVERY and heroism have in all times been extolled, and the praises of the self-sacrificing men and women who have risked their own in the saving of others' lives, been faithfully chronicled.

Railroad men, too long looked upon as the rougher kind of humanity, have been the subjects of severe condemnation and reproach upon the occurrence of every disaster, while their skill, bravery and presence of mind have scarcely ever found a chronicler. The writer ventures to assert, that if the record of their noble deeds were all gathered, and presented in their true light, it would be found that these rough, and weather-worn men were entitled to as high a place, and a fame as lofty, as has been allotted to any other class who cope with disaster.

It has been the aim of the writer, who has shared their dangerous lot, to present a few truthful sketches, trusting that his labor may tend to a better knowledge of the dangers that are passed, by those who drive, and ride behind the IRON HORSE. If he shall succeed in this, and make the time of his reader not appear misspent, he will be satisfied.

CONTENTS.

RUNNING IN A FOG.

RUNNING IN A FOG.

In the year 185– I was running an engine on the ——— road. My engine was named the Racer, and a "racer" she was, too; her driving-wheels were seven feet in diameter, and she could turn them about as fast as was necessary, I can assure you. My regular train was the "Morning Express," leaving the upper terminus of the road at half past four, running sixty-nine miles in an hour and forty-five minutes, which, as I had to make three stops, might with justice be considered pretty fast traveling.

I liked this run amazingly—for, mounted on my "iron steed," as I sped in the dawn of day along the banks of the river which ran beside the road, I saw all nature wake; the sun would begin to deck the eastern clouds with roseate hues—rising higher, it would tip the mountain-tops with its glory—higher still, it would shed its radiance over every hill-side and in every valley. It would illumine the broad bosom of the river, before flowing so dark and drear, now sparkling and glittering with radiant beauty, seeming to run rejoicing in its course to the sea. The little vessels that had lain at anchor all night, swinging idly with the tide, would, as day came on, shake out their broad white sails, and, gracefully careening to the morning breeze, sweep away over the water, looking so ethereal that I no longer wondered at the innocent Mexicans supposing the ships of Cortez were gigantic birds from the spirit-land. Some mornings were not so pleasant, for frequently a dense fog would rise and envelop in its damp, unwholesome folds the river, the road, and all things near them. This was rendered doubly unpleasant from the fact that there were on the line numerous drawbridges which were liable to be opened at all hours, but more especially about day-break. To be sure there were men stationed at every bridge, and in fact every half-mile along the road, whose special duty it was to warn approaching trains of danger from open drawbridges, obstructions on the track, etc., but the class of men employed in such duty was not *noted* for sobriety, and the wages paid were not sufficient to secure a peculiarly intelligent or careful class. So the confidence I was compelled to place in them was necessarily burdened with much distrust.

These men were provided with white and red signal lanterns, detonating torpedoes and colored flags, and the rules of the road required them to place a torpedo on the rail and show a red signal both on the bridge and at a "fog station," distant half a mile from the bridge, before they opened the draw. At all times when the draw was closed they were to show a white light or flag at this "fog station." This explanation will, I trust, be sufficient to enable every reader to understand the position in which I found myself in the "gray" of one September morning.

I left the starting-point of my route that morning ten minutes behind time. The fog was more dense than I ever remembered having seen it. It enveloped every thing. I could not see the end of my train, which consisted of five cars filled with passengers. The "head-light" which I carried on my engine illumined the fleecy cloud only a few feet, so that I was running into the most utter darkness. I did not like the look of things at all, but my "orders" were positive to use all due exertions to make time. So, blindly putting my trust in Providence and the miserable twenty-dollars-a-month-men who were its agents along the road, I darted headlong into and through the thick and, to all mortal vision, impenetrable fog. The Racer behaved nobly that morning; she seemed gifted with the "wings of the wind," and rushed thunderingly on, making such "time" as astonished even me, almost "native and to the manor born." Every thing passed off right. I had "made up" seven minutes of my time, and was within ten miles of my journey's end. The tremendous speed at which I had been running had exhilarated and excited me. That pitching into darkness, blindly trusting to men that I had at best but weak faith in, had given my nerves an unnatural tension, so I resolved to run the remaining ten miles at whatever rate of speed the Racer was capable of making. I gave her steam, and away we flew. The fog was so thick that I could not tell by passing objects how fast we ran, but the dull, heavy and oppressive roar, as we shot through rock cuttings and tunnels, the rocking and straining of my engine, and the almost inconceivable velocity at which the driving-wheels revolved, told me that my speed was something absolutely awful. I did not care, though.

I was used to that, and the rules bore me out; besides, I wanted to win for my engine the title of the fastest engine on the road, which I knew she deserved. So I cried, "*On! on!!*"

I had to cross one drawbridge which, owing to the intervention of a high hill, could not be seen from the time we passed the "fog station" until we were within three or four rods of it. I watched closely for the "fog station" signal. It was white. "All right! go ahead my beauty!" shouted I, giving at the same time another jerk at the "throttle," and we shot into the "cut." In less time than it takes me to write it, we were through, and there on the top of the "draw," dimly seen through a rift in the fog, glimmered with to me actual ghastliness the danger signal—a red light. It seemed to glare at me with almost fiendish malignancy. Stopping was out of the question, even had I been running at a quarter of my actual speed. As I was running, I had not even time to grasp the whistle-cord before we would be in. So giving one longing, lingering thought to the bright world, whose duration to me could not be reckoned in seconds even, I shut my eyes and waited my death, which seemed as absolute and inevitable as inglorious. It was but an instant of time, but an age of thought and dread—and then—I was over the bridge. A drunken bridge-tender had, with accursed stupidity, hoisted the wrong light, and my adventure was but a "*scare*,"—but half a dozen such were as bad as death.

It was three weeks before I ran again, and I never after " made up time " in a fog.

A CLOSE SHAVE.

2

A CLOSE SHAVE.

SEVERAL times during my life I have felt the emotions so often told of, so seldom felt by any man, when, with death apparently absolute and inevitable, immediate and inglorious, staring me full in the face, I forgot all fears for myself—dreamed not of shuddering at the thought that I soon must die—that the gates of death were swung wide open before me, and that, with a speed and force against which all human resistance was useless, I was rushing into them. I knew that I was fated with the rest; but I thought only of those behind me in my charge, under my supervision, then chatting gaily, watching the swift-receding scenery, thinking perhaps how quickly they would be at home with their dear ones, and not dreaming of the hideous panorama of death so soon to unroll, the tinkle of the bell for the starting of which I seemed to hear; the first sad scene, the opening crash of which was sickening my soul with terror and blinding me with despair. For I knew that those voices, now so gay, now so happy, would soon be shrieking in agony, or muttering the dying groan. I knew that those faces, now so smiling, would soon be distorted with pain, or crushed out of all semblance to humanity; and I was powerless to avert the catastrophe. All human force was powerless. Nothing but the hand of God, stretched forth in its Omnipotence, could avert it; and there was scarce time for a prayer for that; for such scenes last but a moment, though their memory endures for all time.

I remember well one instance of this kind. I was running on the R. & W. road, in the East. A great Sabbath-school excursion and picnic was gotten up, and I was detailed to run the train. The children of all the towns on the road were assembled; and, when we got to the grove in which the picnic was to be held, we had eighteen cars full as they could hold of the little ones, all dressed in their holiday attire, and brimful of mirth and gayety. I drew the train in upon the switch, out of the way of passing trains, let the engine cool down, and then went into the woods to participate in the innocent pleasures of the day. The children very soon found out that I was the engineer; and, as I liked children, and tried to amuse them, it was not long before I had a perfect troop at my heels, all laughing and chatting gaily to "Mr. Engineer," as they called me. They asked me a thousand questions about the engine; and one and all tried to extort a promise from me to let them ride with me, several declaring to me in the strictest confidence, their intention of becoming engineers, and their desire, above all things, that I should teach them how.

So the day passed most happily. The children swung in the swings, romped on the grass, picked the flowers, and wandered at their own sweet will all over the woods. A splendid collation was prepared for them, at which I, too, sat down, and liked to have made myself sick eating philopenas with the Billys, Freddys, Mollies, and Matties, whose acquaintance I had made that day, and whose pretty faces and sweet voices would urge me, in a style that I could not find heart to resist, to eat a philopena with them, or "just to taste their cake and see if it wasn't the goodest I ever saw."

But the day passed, as happy or unhappy days will, and time to start came round. We had some trouble getting so many little folks together, and it was only by dint of a great deal of whistling that all my load was collected. I was much amused to see some of the little fellows' contempt at others more timid than they, who shut their ears to the sound of the whistle, and ran to hide in the cars. Innumerable were the entreaties that I had from some of them, to let them ride on the engine, "only this once;" but I was inexorable. The superintendent of the road, who conducted the train, came to me as I was about ready to start, and told me that, as we had lost so much time collecting our load, I had better not stop at the first station, from whence we had taken but a few children, but push on to the next, where we would meet the down train, and send them back from there. Another reason for this was, that I had a heavy train, and it was a very bad stop to make, lying right in a valley, at the foot of two very heavy grades. So, off I started, the children in the cars swinging a dozen handkerchiefs from every window, all happy.

As I had good running-ground, and unless I hurried, was going to be quite late in reaching my journey's end, I pulled out, and let the engine do her best. So we were running very fast—about forty-eight miles an hour. Before arriving at the station at which I was not to stop, I passed through a piece of heavy wood, in the midst of which was a long curve. On emerging from the woods, we left the curve, and struck a straight track, which extended toward the station some forty rods from the woods. I sounded my whistle a half mile from the station, giving a long blow to signify my intention of passing without a stop, and never shut off; for I had a grade of fifty feet to the mile to surmount just as I passed the station, and I wanted pretty good headway to do it with eighteen cars. I turned the curve, shot out into sight of the station, and there saw what almost curdled the blood in my veins, and made me tremble with terror: a dozen cars, heavily laden with stone, stood on the side track, and the switch at this end was wide open! I knew it was useless, but I whistled for brakes, and reversed my engine. I might as well have thrown out a fish-hook and line, and tried to stop by catching the hook in a tree; for, running as I was, and so near the switch, a feather laid on the wheels would have stopped us just as soon as the brakes. I gave up all. I did not think for a moment of the painful death so close to me; I thought only of the load behind me. I thought of their sweet faces, which had so lately smiled on me, now to be distorted with agony, or pale in death. I thought of their lithe limbs, so full of animation, now to be crushed, and mangled, and dabbled in gore. I thought of the anxious parents watching to welcome their smiling, romping darlings home again; doomed, though, to caress only a mangled, crushed, and stiffened corpse, or else to see the fair promises of their young lives blasted forever, and to watch their darlings through a crippled life. 'Twas too horrible. I stood with stiffened limbs and eyeballs almost bursting from their sockets, frozen with terror, and stared stonily and fixedly, as we rushed on—when a man, gifted, it seemed, with super-human strength and activity, darted across the track right in front of the train, turned the switch, and we were saved. I could take those little ones home in

safety! I never run an engine over that road afterwards. The whole thing transpired in a moment; but
a dozen such moments were worse than death, and
would furnish terror and agony enough for a lifetime.

A COLLISION.

A COLLISION.

Of the various kinds of accidents that may befall a railroad-man, a collision is the most dreaded, because, generally, the most fatal. The man who is in the wreck of matter that follows the terrible shock of two trains colliding, stands indeed but a poor chance to escape with either life or limb. No combination of metal or wood can be formed strong enough to resist the tremendous momentum of a locomotive at full or even half speed, suddenly brought to a stand-still; and when two trains meet the result is even more frightful, for the momentum is not only doubled, but the scene of the wreck is lengthened, and the amount of matter is twice as great. The two locomotives are jammed and twisted together, and the wrecked cars stretch behind, bringing up the rear of the procession of destruction. I, myself, never had a collision with another engine, but I did collide with the hind end of another train of forty cars, which was standing still, at the foot of a heavy grade, and into which I ran at about thirty-five miles an hour, and from the ninth car of which I made my way, for the engine had run right into it. The roof of the car was extended over the engine, and the sides had bulged out, and were on either side of me. The cars were all loaded with flour. The shock of the collision broke the barrels open and diffused the " Double Extra Genesee " all over; it mingled with the smoke and steam and floated all round, so that when, during the several minutes I was confined there, I essayed to breathe, I inhaled a compound of flour, dust, hot steam and choking smoke. Take it altogether, that car from which, as soon as I could, I crawled, was a little the hottest, most dusty, and cramped position into which I was ever thrown. To add to the terror-producing elements of the scene, my fireman lay at my feet, caught between the tender and the head of the boiler, and so crushed that he never breathed from the instant he was caught. He was crushed the whole length of his body, from the left hip to the right shoulder, and compressed to the thinness of my hand. In fact, an indentation was made in the boiler where the tender struck it, and his body was between boiler and tender! The way this accident happened was simple, and easily explained. The freight train which I was to pass with the express at the next station, broke down while on this grade. The breakage was trifling and could easily be repaired, so the conductor dispatched a man (a green hand, that they paid twenty-two dollars a month) to the rear with orders, as the night was very dark and rainy, to go clear to the top of the grade, a full mile off, and swing his red light from the time he saw my head light, which he could see for a mile, as the track was straight, until I saw it and stopped, and then he was to tell me what was the matter, and I, of course, would proceed with caution until I passed the train. The conductor was thus particular, for he knew he was a green hand, and sent him back only because he could be spared, in case the train proceeded, better than the other man; and he was allowed only two brakemen. Well, with these apparently clear instructions, the brakeman went back to the top of the grade. I was then in sight; he gave, according to his own statement, one swing of the lamp, and it went out. He had no matches, and what to do he didn't know. He had in his pocket, to be sure, a half a dozen torpedoes, given to him expressly for such emergencies, but if he ever knew their use, he was too big a fool to use the knowledge when it was needed. He might, to be sure, have stood right in the track, and, by swinging his arms, have attracted my attention, for on dark nights and on roads where they hire cheap men, I generally kept a close lookout; and if I saw a man swinging his arms, and, apparently trying to see how like a madman he could act, I stopped quick, for there was no telling what was the matter. But this fellow was too big a fool for that even. He turned from me and made towards his own train, bellowing lustily, no doubt, for them to go ahead, but they were at the engine, and its hissing steam made too much noise for them to hear, even had he been within ten rods of them. But a mile away, that chance was pretty slim, and yet on it hung a good many lives. I came on, running about forty-five miles an hour, for the next station was a wood and water station, and I wanted time there.

I discovered the red light, held at the rear of the train, when within about fifteen rods of it. I had barely time to shut off, and was in the very act of reversing when the collision took place. The tender jumped up on the foot-board, somehow I was raised at the same time, so that it did not catch my feet, but the end of the tank caught my hand on the " reverse lever," which I had not time to let go, and there I was fast. The first five cars were thrown clear to one side of the track, by the impetus of my train ; the other four were crushed like egg-shells, and in the ninth, the engine brought up. I was fast; it all occurred in a second, and the scene was so confusing and rapid that I hardly knew when my hand *was* caught; I certainly should not have known where but for the locality of the piece of it afterwards found. My pain was awful, for not only was my hand caught, but the wood from the tender, as I crouched behind the dome, gave my body a most horrible pummeling, and the blinding smoke and scalding steam added to the misery of my position. I really began to fear that I should have to stay there and undergo the slow, protracted torture of being scalded to death ; but with a final effort I jerked my hand loose, and groped my way out. My clothes were saturated with moisture. The place had been so hot that my hands peeled, and my face was blistered. I did not fully recover for months. But at last I did and went at it again, to run into the doors of death, which are wide open all along every mile of a

3

railroad, and into which, even if nature does not let you go, some fool of a man, who is willing to risk his own worthless neck in such scenes for twenty-five dollars a month, will contrive, ten chances against one, by his stupid blundering to push you.

COLLISION EXTRAORDINARY.

COLLISION EXTRAORDINARY.

One morning, in the year 185–, I was running the Morning Express, or the Shanghæ run, as it was called, on the H. road in New York state. The morning was foggy, damp and uncomfortable, and by its influence I was depressed so that I had the "blues" very badly; I felt weary and tired of the life I was leading, dull and monotonous always, save when varied by horror. I got to thinking of the poor estimate in which the class to which I belonged was held by the people generally, who, seated in the easy-cushioned seats of the train, read of battles far away—of deeds of heroism, performed amid the smoke and din of bloody wars,—and their hearts swell with pride,—they glow with gladness to think that their own species are capable of such daring acts, and all the while these very

(37)

readers are skirting the edges of precipices, to look down which would appall the stoutest heart and make the strongest nerved man thrill with terror;—they are crossing deep, narrow gorges on gossamer-like bridges;—they are passing switches at terrific speed, where there is but an inch of space between smooth-rolling prosperity and quick destruction;—they are darting through dark, gloomy tunnels, which would be turned into graves for them, were a single stone to be detached from the roof in front of the thundering train;—they are dragged by a fiery-lunged, smoke-belching monster, in whose form are imprisoned death-dealing forces the most terrific. And mounted upon this fire-fiend sits the engineer, controlling its every motion, holding in his hand the thread of every life on the train, which a single act—a false move—a deceived eye, an instant's relaxation of thought or care on his part, would cut, to be united nevermore; and the train thunders on, crossing bridges, gullies and roads, passing through tunnels and cuts, and over embankments. The engineer, firm to his post, still regulates the breath of his steam-demon and keeps his eye upon the track ahead, with a thousand things upon his mind, the neglect or a wrong thought of either of which would run the risk of a thousand lives;

—and these readers in the cars are still absorbed with the daring deeds of the Zouaves under the warm sun of Italy, but pay not a thought to the Zouave upon the engine, who every day rides down into the "valley of death" and charges a bridge of Magenta.

But to return to this dismal, foggy morning that I began to tell you of. It was with some such thoughts as these that I sat that morning upon my engine, and plunged into the fog-banks that hung over the river and the river-side. I sat so

"Absorbed in guessing, but no syllable expressing"

of whether it must always be so with me; whether I should always be chilled with this indifference and want of appreciation in my waking hours, and in my sleep have this horrible responsibility and care to sit, ghoul-like, upon my breast and almost stifle the beating of my heart;—when with a crash and slam my meditations were interrupted, and the whole side of the "cab," with the "smoke-stack," "whistle-stand" and "sand-box" were stripped from the engine. The splinters flew around my head, the escaping steam made most an infernal din, and the "fire-box" emitted most as infernal a smoke, and I was entirely ignorant of what was up or the extent of the damage done. As soon as I could stop, I of course, after seeing that every thing was right with the engine, went back to see what was the cause of this sudden invasion upon the dreary harmony of my thoughts, and the completeness of my running arrangements, when lo! and behold it was a North River *schooner* with which I had collided. It had, during the fog, been blown upon the shore, and into its "bowsprit," which projected over the track, I had run full tilt.

I think that I am justified in calling a collision between a schooner on the river and a locomotive on the rail, a *collision extraordinary*. Readers, do not you?

BURNING OF THE HENRY CLAY.

BURNING OF THE HENRY CLAY.

THERE is one reminiscence of my life as a "railroad man" that dwells in my memory with most terrible vividness, one that I often think of in daytime with shuddering horror; and in the night, in dreams of appalling terror, each scene is renewed in all the ghastliness of the reality, so that the nights when I dream of it become epochs of miserable, terrible helplessness.

It was on a clear, bright day in August. The fields were covered with the maturity of verdure, the trees wore their coronal of leaves perfected, the birds sang gaily, and the river sparkled in the sun; and I sat upon my engine, looking ahead mostly, but occasionally casting my eyes at the vessels on the river, that spread their white sails to the breeze and danced over the rippling waters,

(43)

looking too graceful to be of earth. Among the craft upon the river I noticed the steamboat " Henry Clay ;" another and a rival boat was some distance from it, and from the appearance of things I inferred that they were racing. I watched the two as closely as I could for some-time, and while looking intently at the " Clay," I saw a dark column of thick black smoke ascending from her, " amidships," just back of the smoke-pipe. At first I paid little heed to it, but soon it turned to fire, and the leaping flames, like serpents, entwined the whole of the middle portion of the boat in their terrible embrace. She was at once headed for the shore, and came rushing on, trailing the thick cloud of flame and smoke. She struck the shore near where I had stopped my train, for, of course, seeing such a thing about to happen, I stopped to enable the hands and passengers to render what assist-ance they could. The burning boat struck the shore by the side of a little wharf, right where the station of " Riv-erdale" now stands, and those who were upon the forward part of her decks escaped at once by leaping to the shore ; but the majority of the passengers, including all of the women and children, were on the after-part of the boat, and owing to the centre of the boat being entirely en-

wrapped by the hissing flames, they were utterly unable
to get to the shore. So they were cooped up on the ex-
treme after-end of the boat, with the roaring fire forming
an impassable barrier to prevent their reaching the land,
and the swift-flowing river at their feet, surging and bubbling past, dark, deep, and to most of them as certain
death as the flames in front. The fire crept on. It drove
them inch by inch to the water. The strong swimmers,
crazed by the heat, wrapped their stalwart arms about
their dear ones, and leaped into the water. Their mutual
struggles impeded each other; they sank with words of
love and farewell bubbling from their lips, unheard amidst
the roar of the flames and hiss of the water, as the burning timbers fell in and were extinguished. Women raised
their hands to Heaven, uttered one piercing, despairing
scream, and with the flames enwrapping their clothing,
leaped into the stream, which sullenly closed over them.
Some crawled over the guards and hung suspended until
the fierce heat compelled them to loose their hold and drop
into the waves below. Mothers, clasping their children to
their bosoms, knelt and prayed God to let this cup pass
from them. Many, leaping into the water, almost gained
the shore, but some piece of the burning wreck would fall

upon them and crush them down. Some we could see kneeling on the deck until the surging flames and blinding smoke shrouded them and hid them from our sight. One little boy was seen upon the hurricane roof, just as it fell. Entwined in each other's embrace, two girls were seen to rush right into the raging fire, either delirious with the heat or desirous of quickly ending their dreadful sufferings, which they thought *must* end in death. And we upon the shore stood almost entirely powerless to aid. Death-shrieks and despairing cries for help, prayer and blasphemy, all mingled, came to our ear above the roaring and crackling of the flames, and in agony and the terror of helplessness we closed our ears to shut out the horrid sounds. The intense heat of the fire rendered it impossible for us to approach near the boat. The many despairing creatures struggling in the water made it almost certain death for any to swim out to help. No boats were near, except the boats of a sloop which came along just as the fire was at its highest and were unable to get near the wreck, because of the heat. The scene among the survivors was most terrible. One little boy of about seven, was running around seeking his parents and sisters. Poor fellow! his search was vain, for the scorching flames had killed them, and the rapid river had buried them. A mother was there, nursing a dead babe, which drowned in her arms, as, with almost superhuman exertions, she struggled to the shore. A young lady sat by the side of her father, lying stark and stiff, killed by a falling beam, within twenty feet of the shore. A noble Newfoundland dog stood, sole guardian of a little child of three or four, that he had brought ashore himself, and to whom we could find neither kith nor kin among the crowd. His dog, playmate of an hour before, was now the saviour of his life and his only friend. I left the scene with my train when convinced that a longer stay was useless, as far as saving life went.

I returned that afternoon, and the water had given up many of its dead. Twenty-two bodies lay stretched upon the shore—but one in a coffin, and she a bride of that morning, with the wedding-dress scorched and blackened, and clinging with wet, clammy folds to her stiff and rigid form. Her husband bent in still despair over her. A little child lay there, unclaimed. His curly, flaxen hair that, two hours before, father and sisters stroked so fondly, was matted around his forehead, and begrimed with the sand, over which his little body had been washed to the river-bank.   His little lips, that a mother pressed so lately, now were black with the slime of the river-bed in which he went to sleep.   An old man of seventy was there, sleeping calmly after the battle of life, which for him culminated with horror at its close.   In short, of all ages they were there, lying on the sand, and the scene I shall never forget.   Each incident, from the first flashing out of the flame to the moment when I, with reverent hands, helped lay them in their coffins and the tragedy closed, is photographed forever upon my mind.

THE CONDUCTOR.

4

THE CONDUCTOR.

A RECENT case in the courts of this county, has set me to thinking of some of the wrongs heaped upon railroad men so much, that I shall devote this article exclusively to a review of the opprobrium bestowed upon all men connected with railroads, by the people who every day travel under their control, with their lives subject to the care and watchfulness of these men, for whose abuse they leave no opportunity to escape. Does a train run off the track, and thereby mischief be worked, every possible circumstance that can be twisted and distorted into a shape such as to throw the blame upon the men connected with the road, *is* so twisted and distorted. The probability of any accident happening without its being directly caused by the scarcely less than criminal negligence of

(51)

some of the railroad men, is always scouted by the discerning public; most of whom scarcely know the difference between a locomotive and a pumping engine. An accident caused by the breaking of a portion of the machinery of a locomotive engine on the Hudson River Railroad, which did no damage except to cause a three hours' detention, was by some enterprising and intelligent (?) penny-a-liner dignified into a proof of the general incompetency of railroad men, in one of our prominent literary periodicals, and the question was very sagely asked why the railroad company did not have engines that would not break down, or engineers that would not allow them so to do? The question might, with equal propriety, be asked, why did not nature form trees, the timber of which would not rot? Or, why did not nature make rivers that would not overflow?

Let two suits be brought in almost any of our courts, each with circumstances of the same aggravation, say for assault and battery, and let the parties in one be ordinary citizens, and in the other, let one party be a railroad man and the other a citizen, with whom, for some cause, the railroad man has had a difficulty, and you will invariably see the railroad man's case decided against him, and in the other case the defendant be acquitted, to go scot-free. Why is this? Simply, I think, because every individual who has ever suffered from the hands of any railroad employee, treasures up that indignity, and lays it to the account of every other railroad man he meets, making the class suffer in his estimation, because one of them treated him in a crusty manner.

If a man's neighbor or friend offend him, he tries to forgive it—earnestly endeavors to find palliating circumstances; but, in the case of railroad men, all that would palliate the offense of rudeness and want of courtesy, such as is sometimes shown, is studiously ignored, or, at the mildest, forgotten.

I knew a school teacher once, who said that the most barbarous profession in the world was that of teaching, because it drove from a man all humanity. He got into such a habit of ruling, that it became impossible for him to understand how to obey any one himself.

The same thing might be said of a railroad conductor; for, every day in his life, he takes the exclusive control of a train full of passengers of as different dispositions as they are of different countenances. Now, he meets with a testy, quarrelsome old fellow, who is given to fault-finding, and who blows him up at every meeting. Now, with a querulous old maid, who is in continual fear lest the train run off the track, the boiler burst, or the conductor palm off some bad money on her. Now, with a gent of an inquisitive turn of mind, who is continually asking the distance to the next station, and the time the train stops there, or else pulling out an old turnip of a watch and comparing his time with the conductor's. Then, a stupid, dunderheaded man is before him, who does not know where he is going, nor how much money he has got. Then, somebody has got carried by, and scolds the conductor for it, or else angrily insists that the train be immediately backed up for his especial accommodation. The next man, maybe, is an Irishman, made gloriously happy and piggishly independent, by the aid of poor whiskey, who will pay his fare how he pleases, and when he pleases; who is determined to ride where he wants to, and who will at once jump in for a fight, if any of these rights of his are invaded; or, mayhap, he will not pay his fare at all, deeming that his presence (scarcely more endurable than a hog's) is sufficient honor to remunerate the company for his ride; or perhaps his " brother Tiddy, or Pathrick, or Michael, or Dinnis works upon the thrack," and "bedad, he'll jist ride onyway." All these characters are found in any train, and with them the conductor has to deal every day. How do you know, when he speaks harshly to you, but that he has just had a confab with one of these gentry, who has sorely tried his patience, and riled his temper? How do you think you would fill his place, were you subjected to such annoyances all the time? Would you be able at all times to maintain a perfectly correct and polite exterior—a Christian gravity of demeanor—and never for an instant forget yourself, or lose your temper, or allow your manner to show to any one the slightest acerbity? You know you could not; and yet, for being only thus human, you are loud in your denunciation of conductors and all railroad men, and, perhaps honestly, but certainly with great injustice, believe them to have no care for your wants, no interest in your comfort. Treat railroad men with the same consideration that you evince towards other business companions. Consider always that they are only human —have not saintly nor angelic tempers, any of them, and that every day's experience is one of trial and provocation. By so doing, you will be only rendering them simple justice, and you will yourself receive better treatment than if you attempt to make the railroad man your menial, or the pack-horse for all your ill-feeling.

BRAVERY OF AN ENGINEER.

BRAVERY OF AN ENGINEER.

THE presence of mind shown by railroad men is a great deal talked about; but few, I think, know the trying circumstances under which it must be exercised, because they have never thought of, and are not familiar enough with the details of the business, and the common, every-day incidents of the lives of railroad men. If any thing does happen to a train of cars, or an engine, it comes so suddenly, and is all over so quickly, that the impulse, and effort, to do something to prevent it, must be instantaneous, or they are of no avail. The mind must devise, and the hands spring to execute at once, for the man is on a machine that moves like the wind-blast, and will snap bands and braces of iron or steel as easily as the wild horse would break a halter of thread.

(59)

The engine, while under the control of its master, moves along regularly and with the beauty of a dream; its wheels revolve, glancing in the sun; its exhausted steam coughs as regularly as the strong man's heart beats, and trails back over the train, wreathing itself into the most fantastic convolutions; now sweeping away towards the sky in a grand, white pillar, anon twining and twisting among the gnarled limbs of the trees beside the track, and the train moves on so fast that the scared bird in vain tries to get out of its way by flying ahead of it. Still the engineer sits there cool and calm; but let him have a care,—let not the exhilaration of his wild ride overcome his prudence, for the elements he controls are, while under his rule, useful and easily managed, but broken loose, they have the power of a thousand giants, and do the work of a legion of devils in almost a single beat of the pulse.

A man can easily retain his presence of mind where the danger depends entirely upon him; that is, where his maintaining one position, or doing one thing resolutely, will avert the catastrophe; but under circumstances such as frequently beset an engineer, where, to do his utmost, he can only partially avert the calamity, then it is that the natural bravery and acquired courage of a man is tried to the utmost extent. I remember several instances of this kind, where engineers, in full view of the awful danger which threatened them, knowing too well the terrible chances of death that were against them and the passengers under their charge, even if they did maintain their positions, and, by using all their exertions, succeeded in slightly reducing the shock of the collision, which could only be modified—not averted—still stuck to their posts, did their utmost, and rode into the other train and met their death, amid the appalling scenes of the chaotic ruin which followed.

George D—— was running the Night Express on the —— road. I was then running the freight train, which laid over at a station for George to pass. One night—it was dark and dismal—the rain had been pouring down in torrents all night long; I arrived with my train, went in upon the switch and waited for George, who passed on the main track without stopping. Owing to the storm and the failure of western connections, George was some thirty minutes behind, and of course came on, intending to run though the station pretty fast—a perfectly safe proceeding, apparently, for the switches could not be turned wrong without changing the lights, and these be-

ing " bull's-eye" lanterns elevated so that they could be
seen a great distance on the straight track which was
there, no change could be made without the watchful eye
of the engineer seeing it at once.   So George came on, at
about thirty-five miles an hour, as near as I could judge,
and I was watching him all the time.   He was within
about three times the length of his train of the switch—
was blowing his whistle—when I saw, and *he* saw the
switchman run madly out of his " shanty," grab the switch
and turn it so that it would lead him directly into the hind
end of my train.   I jumped, instinctively, to start my engine—I heard him whistle for brakes, and those that stood
near said that he reversed his engine—but my train was too
heavy for me to move quickly, and he was too near to do
much good by reversing, so I soon felt a heavy concussion, and knew that he had struck hard, for, at the other
end of forty-five cars, it knocked me down, and the jar
broke my engine loose from the train.   He might have
jumped from his engine with comparative safety, after he
saw the switch changed, for the ground was sandy there
and free from obstructions ; and he could easily have
jumped clear of the track and escaped with slight bruises.
But no!   Behind him, trusting to him, and resting in

comparative security, were hundreds to whom life was as dear as to him; his post was at the head; to the great law of self-preservation, that most people put first in their code of practice, his stern duty required him to forswear allegiance, and to act on the principle, "others first, myself afterwards." So, with a bravery of heart such as is seldom found in other ranks of men, he stuck to his iron steed, transformed then into the white steed of death, and spent the last energies of his life, the strength of his last pulse, striving to mitigate the suffering which would follow the collision. His death was instantaneous; he had no time for regrets at leaving life and the friends he loved so dearly. When we found him, one hand grasped the throttle, his engine was reversed, and with the other hand he still held on to the handle of the sand-box lever. The whole middle and lower portion of his body was crushed, but his head and arms were untouched, and his face still wore a resolute, self-sacrificing expression, such as must have lit up the countenance of Arnold Winkleried, when crying, "*Make way for liberty*," he threw himself upon a sheaf of Austrian spears and broke the column of his enemies.

I find in nearly every cemetery that I visit, monuments

and memorial-stones to some brave man who fell and died amid the smoke and flame and hate of a battle-field; and orators and statesmen, ministers and newspapers, exhaust the fountains of eloquence to extol the "illustrious dead." But George D——, who spent his life in a constant bat tle with the elements, who waged unequal war with time and space, who at last chose rather to die himself than to bring death or injuries to others, sleeps in the quiet of a country church-yard. The wailing wind, sighing through the few trees there, sings his only dirge; a plain stone, bought by the hard won money of his companions in life, alone marks his resting-place. The stranger, passing by, would scarcely notice it; but who shall dare to tell me that there resteth not there a frame, from which a soul has flown, as noble as any that sleeps under sculptured urn or slab, over which thousands have mused, and which has been the text of hundreds of exhortations to patriotism and self-forgetfulness?

ONE OF THE THREE ENGINES FIRST BUILT BY STEPHENSON,
And used on the Stockton and Darlington Railway.

THE FIREMAN.

5

THE FIREMAN.

THE fireman, the engineer's *left*-hand man, his trump card, without whom it would be difficult for him to get over the road, is seen but little, and thought but little of. He is usually dirty and greasy, wearing a ragged pair of overalls, originally blue, but now embroidered so with oil and dust, that they are become a smutty brown. Just before the train leaves the station, you will see his face, down which streams the perspiration, looking back, watching for the signal to start; for this is one of his many duties. His head is usually ornamented (in his opinion) with some outlandish cap or hat; though others regard it as a fittingly outrageous cap-sheaf to his general dirty and outre appearance. But little cares Mr. Fireman; he runs the fire-box of that "machine." He feels pride in the whole engine; and when he sees any one admiring its polished surface, gleaming so brightly in the sun, flashing so swiftly by the farm-houses on the road (in each of which Mr. Fireman has acquaintance of the opposite sex, to whom he must needs swing his handkerchief), he feels a glow of honest satisfaction; and the really splendid manner in which his efforts have caused it to shine— which is evidently one great reason for the admiration bestowed upon it—so fills him with self gratulation that, in his great modesty, which he fears will be overcome if he stays there much longer watching people as they admire his handiwork, and he be led to tell them all about it, how he scrubbed and scoured to bring her to that pitch of perfection—he turns away, and begins to pitch the wood about in the most reckless manner imaginable; yet every stick goes just where he wants it.

His aspirations (and he has them, my lily-handed friend, as well as you, and perhaps, though not so elevated, more honorable than yours) are, that he may, by attending to his own duties, so attract the attention of the ones in authority that he may be placed in positions where he can learn the business, and, by and by, himself have charge of an engine as its runner. It does not seem a very high ambition; but, to attain it, he undergoes a probation seldom of less than three, frequently of seven or eight years, at the hardest kind of work, performed, too, where dangers are thick around him, and his chances to avert them very slim. . His duties are manifold and various; but long years of attendance to them makes them very monotonous and irksome, and he would soon weary of them, did not the hope of one day being himself sole master of the "iron horse," actuate him to renewed diligence and continued efforts to excel. He is on duty longer than any other man connected with the train. He must be on hand before the engine comes out of the shop, to start a fire and see that all is right about the engine. Usually he brings it out upon the track; and then, when all is ready, he begins the laborious work of throwing wood; which amounts to the handling of from four to seven cords of wood per diem, while the engine and tender are pitching and rolling so that a "green-horn" would find it hard work to stand on his feet, let alone having, while so standing, to keep that fiery furnace supplied with fuel. The worse the day, the more the snow or rain blows, the harder his work. His hands become calloused with the numerous wounds he receives from splinters on the wood. He it is who has to go out on the runboard and oil the valves, while the engine is running full speed. No matter how cold the wind may blow, how rain, hail, sleet, or snow may beat down upon him, covering every thing with ice, nor how dark the night, out there he must go and crawl along the slippery side of the engine to do his work. At stations he must take water, and when at last the train arrives at its destination, and others are ready to go home, he must stay. If a little too much wood is in the fire-box, he must take it out, and then go to work cleaning and scouring the dust and rust from off the bright work and from the boiler. Every bit of cleaning in the cab and above the runboard, including the cylinders and steam-chest, must be done by him; and any one who will look at the fancy-work on some of our modern loco-motives, can judge something of what he has to do after the day's work on the road is done. Every thing is brass, or covered with brass; and all must be kept polished like a mirror, or the fireman is hauled over the coals.

For performing these manifold duties, he receives the magnificent sum of (usually) thirty dollars per month; and he knows no Sundays, no holidays—on long roads, he scarcely knows sleep. He has not the responsibility rest-ing on him that there is upon the engineer; but it is required of him, when not otherwise engaged with his duty of firing, to assist the engineer in keeping a lookout ahead. His position is one of the most dangerous on the train, as is proved by the frequent occurrence of accidents, where only the fireman is killed ; and his only obituary, no matter how earnest he may have been, how faithful in the performance of his duties, is an item in the telegraphic reports, that *a fireman was killed* in such a railroad smash. He may have been one of nature's noblemen. A fond mother and sweet sisters may have been dependent on his scanty earnings for their support. No matter ; the great surging tide of humanity that daily throngs these avenues of travel, has not time to inquire after, nor sympathy to waste upon, a greasy wood-passer, whom they regard as simply a sort of piece in the machinery of the road, not half so essential as a valve or bolt, for if he be lost, his place can be at once supplied ; but if a bolt or other essential piece of the iron machinery give out, it will most likely cause a vexatious delay. Once in a while a fireman performs some heroic act that brings him into a momentary notoriety, and opens the eyes of the few who may be cognizant of the case, to the fact that, on a railroad, all men are in danger, and that the most humble of them may perform some self-sacrificing deed that will, at the expense of his own, save many other lives.

In a collision that occurred at a station on one of the roads in New York state, the engineer, a relative of some of the managers of the road, who had fired only half so long as the man then firing for him, jumped from the engine, leaving it to run at full speed into the hind end of a train standing on a branch track, of which the switch was wrong; not doing a single thing to avert or mitigate the calamity; fearing only for his own precious neck, which a hemp cravat would ornament, to the edification of the world. The fireman sprang at once to the post vacated by the engineer, reversed the engine, opened the sand-box valve, and rode into the hind end of that train; losing, in so doing, a leg and an arm. He has been most munificently rewarded for his heroism, being now employed to attend a crossing and hold a flag for passing trains, and receiving the princely compensation of twenty-five dollars per month; while the engineer, who deserted his post and left all to *kind Providence*, is running on the road at a salary of seventy-five per month.

THE BRAKEMAN.

THE BRAKEMAN.

A VERY humble class of railroad men, a class that gets poorer pay in proportion to the work they do and the dangers they run than any other upon a road, are the brakemen. Though perhaps less responsibility rests upon them, they are placed in the most dangerous position on the train; they are expected to be at their posts at all times, and to flinch from no contingency which may arise. The managers of a railroad expect and demand the brakemen to be as prompt in answering the signals of the engineer as the throttle-valve is obedient to his touch.

Reader, were you ever on a train of cars moving with the wings of the wind, skimming over the ground as rapidly as a bird flies, darting by tree and house, through cuttings and over embankments? and did you ever feel a

(75)

sudden jar that almost jerked you from your seat? At the same time did you hear a sharp, sudden blast of the whistle, ringing out as if the hand that pulled it was nerved by the presence of danger, braced by a terrible anxiety to avoid destruction? It frightened you, did it not? But did you notice the brakeman then? He rushed madly out of the cars as if he thought the train was going to destruction surely, and he wished, before the crash came, to be out of it. No, that was not his object. He caught hold of the brakes and, with all the force and energy he was capable of exerting, applied them to the swift-revolving wheels, and when you felt the gradual reduction of the speed under the pressure of the brakes, you began to feel easier. But what thought the brakeman all the time? Did he think that, if the danger ahead was any one of a thousand which might happen? if another train was coming towards them, and they should strike it? if a disabled engine was on the track, and a fool, to whom the task was intrusted, had neglected to give your train the signal? if the driving rain had raised some little stream, or a spark of fire had lodged in a bridge and the bridge was gone? if some loosened rock had rolled down upon the track; or if the track had slid;

or if some wretch, wearing a human form over a hellish
soul, had lifted a rail, placed a tie on the track, to hurl engine and car therefrom ?—if any of these things were
ahead and the speed of your train be too great to stop,
and go plunging into it, did he realize that he was the
first man to be caught; that those two cars between
which he stood, straining every nerve to do his share to
avert the catastrophe, would come together and crush him,
as he would crush a worm beneath his tread ?   If he did,
he was doing his duty in that dangerous place, risking his
life at a pretty cheap rate—a dollar a day—wasn't he ?
And still these men do this every day for the same price
and at the same risk, while the passengers regard them as
necessary evils, who *will* be continually banging the doors.
So they pass them by, never giving them a kind word,
scarcely ever thanking them for the many little services
which they unhesitatingly demand of them, and, if the
passenger has ridden long, and the jolting and jarring,
the want of rest, or wearisome monotony of the long ride
has made him peevish, how sure he is to vent his spite on
the brakeman, because he thinks him the most humble,
and therefore the most unprotected man on the train.
And the brakeman endures it all; for if he answers back

a word, if he asserts his manhood—which many seem to think he has sold for his paltry thirty dollars a month— why, he is reported at the office, a garbled version of the affair is given, and the brakeman is discharged.

But have a care, O! most chivalrous passenger, you who fly into such a passion if your dignity is offended by a short answer. You may quarrel with a man having a soul in him beside which yours would look most pitifully insignificant; one who, were the dread signal to sound, would rush out into the danger, and, throwing himself into the chasm, die for you, amid all the appalling scenes of the chaotic wreck of that train of cars, as coolly, as determinately, as unselfishly as the Stuart queen barred the door with her own fair arm, that her liege lord might escape. And then, methinks, you would feel sad when you saw his form stretched there dead, all life crushed out of it—once so comely, now so mangled and unsightly— and thought that, with that poor handful of dust from which the soul took flight so nobly, you had just been picking a petty quarrel.

If you have read the accounts of railroad accidents as carefully and with such thrilling interest as I have, you will remember many incidents where brakemen were killed while at their post, discharging their duty. Several have come under my immediate observation. On the H. R. R. one night I was going over the road, "extra," that is, I was not running the engine, but riding in the car. I heard a sharp whistle, but thought it was not of much consequence, for I knew the engineer's long avowed intention, to never call the brakemen to their posts when the danger could be avoided; he said he would give them a little chance, not call them where they had none. The brakemen all sprang to their posts; the one in the car where I was I saw putting on his brake; the next instant, with a shock that shook every thing loose and piled the seats, passengers, stove, and pieces of the roof all into a mass in the forward end of the car, the engine struck a rock, the cars were all piled together, and I was pitched into the alley up close to the end which was all stove in. I felt blood trickling on my hands, but thought it was from a wound I had received on my head. I soon found that it was from Charley McLoughlin, the brakeman with whom I had just been talking, and whom I saw go to his post at the first signal of danger. The whole lower part of his body was crushed, but he yet lived. We got him out as soon as possible and laid him beside the track on a door, then went to get the rest of the dead and wounded. We found one of the brakemen dead, his head mashed flat; the other one, Joe Barnard, was hurt just as Charley was, and as they were inseparable companions, we laid them together. I took their heads in my lap—we did not try to move them, as the physicians said they could not live—and there for four long hours I sat and talked with those men whose lives were surely, but slowly ebbing away. In life they were as brothers, and death did not separate them, for they departed within fifteen minutes of each other. But notice this fact—the brakeman who was found dead, still held in his hand the shattered brake-wheel, and Joe Barnard was crushed with both hands still grasping his. Yet these men were " only brakemen ! "

A DREAM IN THE "CABOOSE."

6

A DREAM IN THE "CABOOSE."

A FIRST thought of the life of an engineer would be that it was a life peculiarly exhilarating; that in the mind of an engineer the rush and flow of strong feeling and emotion would constantly be felt; that the every-day incidents of his life would keep his nerves continually on the stretch, and that lassitude would never overtake him. But such is not the case. I know of no life that a man could live which would more certainly produce stagnation than it. Every day, in sunshine or storm, cold or heat, light or darkness, he goes through the same scenes, bearing the same burdens of care and responsibility, facing the same dangers, braving grim death ever and all the time until he loses fear, and the novelty of the at first exhilarating effort to conquer space and distance, and make time of no account, wears away, till danger becomes monotonous, and only an occasional scene of horror checkers the unchanging current of his every-day life. He knows every tie on the road; he knows that here is a bad curve, there a weak bridge, from either of which he may at any time, by the most probable of possibilities, be hurled to his death; and still every day he rides his "iron horse," of fiery heart and demon pulse, over the weak places and the strong, posted at the very front of the procession, which any one of a thousand contingencies would make a funeral train. He passes the same stations, blows his whistle at the same point, sees the same men at work in the same fields, with the same horses that they used last year and the year before. Two lines of iron stretch before him, to demand and receive his earnest scrutiny every day, precisely as they have every day for years.

He meets the same men on other trains at the same places, and bids them "hail" and "good-bye" with the same uncertainty of ever seeing them again that he has always felt, and which has grown so sadly wearisome.

He alone knows and appreciates the chances against him, but his daily bread depends upon his running them, so with a resolute will that soon gets to be the merest trusting to luck, he goes ahead, controlled by the same rules, which always have the same dreary penalties attached to them when violated,—a maimed and disfigured body for the balance of his days, or a sudden and inglorious death.

If one of his intimate companions gets killed, he can only bestow a passing thought upon it, for he has not been unexpectant of it, and he knows full well that the same accident may at the same place make it his turn next, as he passes over the same road every day, running the same chances, as did his friend just gone.

I had, while I was on the H—— road, a particular friend, an engineer. We were inseparable, and were both of us, alike, given to fits of despondency, at which times we would, with choking dread, bid each other farewell, and "hang around" the telegraph office to hear the welcome " O K" from the various stations, signifying that our trains had passed " on time" and " all right."

One Saturday night, when my engine was to " lay over" for the Sunday at the upper end of the road, I determined to go back to N——. The only train down that night, was the one o'clock " night freight," which Charley, my friend, was to tow with the " Cumberland," a heavy, clumsy " coal-burner." I went to the engine-house, and

sat down with Charley, to smoke and talk till his "leaving time" came. He had the blues that night, and
after we had talked awhile, I had them too. So we sat
there slowly puffing our pipes, recalling gloomy tales of
our own, and of others' experience; telling of unlucky
engines (a favorite superstition with many engineers),
and of unlucky men, and of bad places on the road, weak
bridges, loose rails, shelving rocks, and bad curves, until
we had got ourselves into the belief that nothing short of
a miracle could possibly enable even a hand-car to pass
over the road in any thing like safety. Had any of the
passengers who daily passed over the road, in the comparative safety of its sumptuous coaches, been there and heard
our description of the road, I guess they would have tak-
en lodgings at the nearest hotel, sooner than have ridden
over the road that night, towed by that engine, which
Charley had more than once characterized as a "death-
trap" and "man-killer," and proven her right to the
name by alluding to the four men she had killed. At
length the hours had dragged themselves along, and the
"Cumberland" was coupled to the train. As I started
for the "Caboose," Charley said to me, "The 'Cumberland' always was and always will be an unlucky

engine, and blamed if I know but she will kill me to-night, so let's shake hands, and good-bye." We shook hands, and I clambered into the " Caboose," having, it must be confessed, a sneaking kind of good feeling to think that I was at the rear instead of the front end of those forty cars, especially as the engine was one that, despite my reason and better judgment, I more than half-believed was " cursed" with " ill-luck;" by which I mean, she was peculiarly liable to fatal accidents. Well, I curled myself up on one of the seats and prepared for sleep; not, though, in just the frame of mind I would choose in order to secure " pleasant slumbers" and " sweet dreams." At first my sleep was fitful; the opening of the door, as the hands frequently went out or came in; the cessation of the jar and rumble when the train stopped; the changing of position as I tossed about in my fitful sleep—these all would wake me. At last, however, I dropped to sleep, and slept long and soundly. Strange dreams, fraught with terror, filled with wild and fantastic objects, danced over and controlled my mind. I was placed in positions of the most awful dread; I was on engines of inconceivable power, powerless to control them, and they ran with the velocity of light into long trains laden with smiling women and romping children, whose shrieks mingled with the curses of their husbands and fathers, who said it was my fault, and cursed me to lingering tortures. Then the scene would change. I would be on a long straight track, mounted on an engine which seemed a devil broken loose, and bent on a mission of death which I could not stir to stop; while away in the distance was another engine, coming towards me, and I felt, by intuition, that it was Charley, and then I would see his white and pallid face, clammy with the sweat of terror, and his long black hair swept back from his forehead, while agony, despair, and the miserable, hopeless fear of instant and horrible death shone with lurid, fierce, unnatural fire from his dark blue eye, and I seemed to know that every one I held dear was on his train; that my sisters were there looking out of the window, gaily laughing and watching for the next station, where my train was to meet theirs, and my mother sat smilingly by, looking on, while other friends that I loved were saying kind words of me, who, in another instant, would be upon them with a fiendish, fiery engine of death. I would shut my eyes, and the

scene would change again. I would be skirting the edges
of deep, dark precipices, and while I looked, shuddering,
down into the dark and sombre depths, my whole train
would go over the bank and down, down—still farther
down it plunged—till I seemed to have gone far enough
for the nether depths. A sudden tremendous jar woke
me, and I sprang to my feet from the floor to which I had
been hurled, and found myself in utter darkness. For
an instant I did not know where I was, but I soon re-
called myself and started out of the "Caboose," fully
convinced that some awful calamity had happened to the
train, and bound to know, in the shortest possible time,
whether Charley or any of the rest of the hands were
hurt. I soon saw a light, and hallooed to know what was
the matter. "Nothing," answered Charley's well-known
voice. "Well," says I, "you make a deuce of a fuss doing nothing." I told him how I was awakened, and we
started back to see what was the matter. We found that,
in throwing the "Caboose" in upon the branch track, he
had given it too much headway, and there being no brakeman on it to check its speed, it had hit the tie laid across
the rail with sufficient force to throw me from the seat

and put out the only lamp in the car. So we went home, laughing heartily ; but I never prepared myself for another midnight ride in the "Caboose" of a freight train by telling horrid stories just before I started.

AN UNMITIGATED VILLAIN.

AN UNMITIGATED VILLAIN.

EVERYBODY knows mean men. Everybody knows people that they think are capable of any mean act, who would, did opportunity present itself, steal, lie, cheat, swear falsely, or do any other act which is vicious. But do any of my readers think that they know any one who would be guilty of deliberately placing an obstruction on a railroad track, over which he knew that a train, laden with human passengers, must soon pass? Yet such men are plenty. Such acts are frequently done, and often with the sole view of stealing from the train during the excitement which must necessarily ensue after such an accident. Sometimes such deeds are done from pure revenge, because the man who does it imagines that the railroad company has done him some injury, and he thinks that by so doing he will reap a rich harvest of vengeance. What kind of a soul can such a man have? The man who desires to steal, wishes to get a chance to do so when people's minds are so occupied with some other idea that their property is not thought of. So he goes to the railroad track and lifts up a rail, places a tie or a T rail across the track, or does something that he thinks will throw the train from the track; and then lies in wait for the accident to happen, calmly and with deliberate purpose awaiting the event; expecting, amid the carnage which will probably follow, to reap his reward; calculating, when it comes, to fill his pockets with the money thus obtained; and when it does happen, and the heavy train, in which, resting in security, are hundreds of passengers, goes off the track, is wrecked, and lies there with every car shattered, and out of their ruins are creeping the mangled victims, who rend the air with their horrid shrieks and moans of agony; when the dead and the mangled are mixed up amidst the appalling wreck; when little children, scarce able to go alone, are so torn to pieces that they linger only for a few moments on earth; when families, that a few moments before were unbroken and happy, are separated forever by the death of the father who lies in sight of the remaining ones, a crushed and bleeding mass, or by the loss of the mother, who, caught by some portion of the wreck, is held, and there, in awful agony, slowly frets her life away, right in sight of all that are dear to her; or, maybe, a husband, who is hurrying home to his dear one lying at the point of death, and anxiously awaiting his coming, that, before she dies, she may bid him good-bye, he is caught and mangled so that he cannot move farther, and the wife dies alone. Maybe a child, long time absent, is hastening home to meet the aged mother or father, and bid them good-bye ere the long running sands are run out entirely; but here he is caught, and his last breath of life goes out with a heart-rending, horrible scream of agony, and only his mangled corpse can go home. All ties may be rudely sundered. The infant at its mother's breast may be killed, and its mother clasp its tiny, bleeding form to her bosom, but it shall smile on her nevermore; its cooing voice shall not welcome her care again on earth. The mother too may be killed, and the moaning child may sob and sigh for the accustomed kiss, but all in vain. The mother, mangled and slain, only holds the child in the stiff embrace of death. The author of it all—where is he? he that did the deed? Is he rummaging the baggage or the pockets of the dead to find spoil? If he is, surely every cent he gets will blister his fingers through all time and in hell. The wail of the dying and the last gasp of the dead will, through all time, surely ring in his ears with horrible distinctness, and with a sound ominous of eternal torture. The horrible sight of the mangled, bleeding bodies, the set eyes, and jaws locked from excessive torture, will surely fasten on his eye forever, and blister his sight. Horrid dreams, wherein jibing fiends shall mock at him and the wail of the damned ring forever in his ears, shall surely visit his pillow and haunt him every night. Each voice that he hears amid the carnage shall seem, in after-time, to be the voice of an accusing angel telling him of his guilt.

So we would think, and yet men do it. Some in order to have a chance to steal, others as revenge for some petty injury; and they live, and, if detected, are sent for ten or twenty years to the penitentiary, as if that were punishment enough! It may be that I feel too strongly on the subject, but it seems to me that an eternity in hell would scarce be more than sufficient punishment for such a damnable deed. I think I could coolly and without compunction tread the drop to launch such a being to eternity; for surely no good influence that earth affords would be sufficient to reclaim such a man from the damnable depravity of his nature. Surely a man capable of such a deed, is a born fiend fit only for the abiding place of the accursed of God, whose voice should ever be heard howling in sleepless, eternal agony in the sulphurous chambers of the devil's home. I do feel strongly on this subject, for I have stood by and seen many a horrid death of this kind; I have held the hands of dear friends and felt their last convulsive pressure amid such scenes, whose deaths were caused by the diabolical malignity of some devil, who, for the nonce, had assumed human shape, and in revenge for the death of a cow, or for the unpaid occupation of land, or to get a chance to rob, had placed something on the track and thrown the cars therefrom. I have seen things placed on the track, rails torn up, and other traps, the ingenuity of whose arrangement could only have been begotten by the devil; and I have shut my eyes and thought that I had taken my last look at earth and all its glories; but I have escaped. I never caught one of these wretches, and I never want to; for if I should, I am afraid I would become an instrument for ridding the earth of a being who had secured good title (and could not lose it) to an abode in the nethermost hell.

7

A PROPOSED RACE

STEAM AND LIGHTNING.

A PROPOSED RACE BETWEEN STEAM AND LIGHTNING.

OLD Wash. S—— is known by almost every railroad engineer, at least by reputation. A better engineer, one who could make better time, draw heavier loads, or keep his engine in better repair, I never knew. But Wash. had one failing, he would drink; and if he was particularly elated with any good fortune, or was expecting to make a fast run, he was sure to get full of whiskey; and though in that state never known to transgress the rules of the road by running on another train's time, or any thing of that sort, still he showed the thing which controlled him by running at a terrible rate of speed. At one time they purchased a couple of engines for the E. road, on which Wash. was running. These engines were very large, and were intended to be very fast, being put

(101)

up on seven feet wheels. From the circumstance of their being planked between the spokes of their " drivers," that is, having a piece of plank set in between the spokes, the " boys " used to call them the " plank-roaders." They were tried, and though generally considered capable of making " fast time " under favorable circumstances, they didn't suit that road; so they were condemned to " the gravel-pit," until they could receive an overhauling, and be " cut down " a foot or two. Wash. had always considered that these engines were much abused, and had never received fair treatment; so he obtained permission of the Superintendent to take one of them into the shop · and repair it. At it he went, giving the engine a thorough overhauling, fixing her valves for the express purpose of running fast, and making many alterations in minor portions of her machinery. At last he had the job completed, and took her out on the road. After running one or two trips on freight trains to smooth her brasses, and try her working, he was " chalked " for the fastest train on the road, the B. Express. All the " boys " on the road were anxious for the result, for it was expected that " Old Wash." and the " plank-roader " would " astonish the natives," that trip. Wash. imbibed rather freely, and was somewhat under the influence of liquor when the leaving time of his train came, though not enough to be noticed; but as minute after minute passed, and the train with which it connected did not make its appearance, Wash., who kept drinking all the time, grew tighter and tighter, till at last, when it did come in, an hour and a half "behind time," Wash. was pretty comfortably drunk; so much so that some of the men who had to go on the train with him looked rather "skeery," for they knew that they might expect to be "towed" as fast as the engine could run. How fast that was no one knew, but her seven feet wheels promised a near approach to flying.

At last they started, and I freely confess that I never took as fast a ride in my life. (Wash. had got me to fire for him.) Keeping time was out of the question as far as I was concerned, for I had my hands full to keep the "fire-box" full, and hold my hat on. We had not run more than ten miles, before the brakemen, ordered by the conductor, put on the brakes, impeding our speed somewhat, but not stopping us, for we were on a heavy down grade, and Wash. had her "wide open," and working steam at full stroke. At last the conductor came over and begged Wash. not to run so fast, for the passengers were half scared out of their senses. Wash. simply pointed to the directions to use all " due exertion" to make up time, and never shut off a bit. So on we flew to B., forty miles from where we started, and the first stopping place for the train. Here the conductor came to Wash. again and told him if he did not run slower, the passengers were going to leave. Wash. said, " Let them leave," and gave no promises. Some of them did leave, so also did one of the brakemen, and the baggageman, but away we went without them to O., where a message from head-quarters was awaiting us, telling them to take Wash. from the engine and put another man on in his place. I told him of the message, and picking up his coat, he got off and staggered to a bench on the stoop of the depot, where he laid down, seemingly to sleep. I started back to the engine, but Wash. called after me, and asked me " how we got the orders to take him off?" I told him " by telegraph." "Humph," said he, rolling over, " *wish I'd known that, the confounded dispatch never should have passed me!*"

Wash. of course was not reinstated, but the " plank-roader" never made the running time of any of the fast trains with any other man on the " foot-board."

AN ABRUPT "CALL."

AN ABRUPT "CALL."

"HI WHITE," as he was familiarly called, was an engineer on the same road with me. He has been running there for over ten years, and, although Hi is one of those mad wags who are never so happy as when " running a rig " on some of their cronies, he was universally acknowledged to be one of the most competent and careful men that ever " pulled a plug " on a locomotive.

In Hi's long career as a runner, he, of course, has met with innumerable hair-breadth 'scapes; some of them terribly tragic in their accessories; others irresistibly comic in their termination, although commencing with fair prospect for a fearful end. Of this latter kind was an adventure of his, which he used to call " making a morning call under difficulties." Hi used to run the

Morning Express, or, as it was called, the " Shanghae
run," which left the Southern terminus of the road at 6
o'clock A.M.   It was a " fast run," making the length
of the road (one hundred and forty-one miles) in three
and a half hours.   Hi ran the engine Columbia, a
fast " machine," with seven feet driving wheels, and a
strong inclination to mount the rail and leave the track on
the slightest provocation.   About midway of the road
there was a large brick house, standing but a rod or two
from the track and on the outside of a sharp curve.   As
Hi was passing the curve one day, running at full
speed, some slight obstruction caused the Columbia to
leave the track, breaking the coupling between it and the
train, thus leaving the cars on the track.   Away went the
Columbia, making the gravel fly until she met with an
obstruction in the shape of this very brick house, which
the engine struck square in the broad-side, and, with
characteristic contempt of slight obstacles, crashed its way
through the wall and on to the parlor floor, which, being
made for lighter tread, gave way and precipitated the engine into the cellar beneath, leaving only the hind end of
the tender sticking out of the breach in the wall.   Hi, who
had jumped off at the first symptom of this furious on-

slaught, looked to see if there were any dead or wounded on the field of this " charge of his heavy brigade." Seeing that he and his fireman were both safe, he turned his attention to the Columbia, which he found " slightly injured but safely housed," lying coolly among pork barrels, apple bins and potato heaps, evidently with no present probability of continuing its course. By this time the people of the house, who were at breakfast in the farther part of the building when the furious incursion upon their domestic economy took place, came rushing out, not knowing whether to prepare to meet friend or rebel foe. Very naturally the first question put to Hi (who was renewing vegetable matter for present rumination, i. e. taking a new chew of tobacco), was, " What's the matter?" This question was screamed to Hi, with the different intonations of the various members of the family. Hi coolly surveyed the frightened group and replied, " Matter—nothing is the matter. I only thought I would call on you this morning, and pray," said he, with the most winning politeness, " *don't put yourself to any trouble on my account.*"

THE GOOD LUCK OF BEING OBSTINATE.

8

THE GOOD LUCK OF BEING OBSTINATE.

I THINK people generally look upon railroad men as a distinct species of the *genus homo*. They seem to regard them as a class who have the most utter disregard for human life, as perfectly careless of trusts imposed upon them, and as being capable of distinctly understanding rules the most obscure, and circumstances the most complicated. They seem to think a railroad man is bound to make time any way, in the face of every difficulty, and to hold him absolutely criminal if he meets with any accident, or fails to see his way safe out of any trouble into which their urging may force him. My impression is that they are wrong, that railroad men have but human courage, but human foresight, and should be spared the most of the indiscriminate censure heaped upon them when an accident happens.

If one were to judge from the words of the press and the finding of coroners' juries, he would infer that a pure accident, one unavoidable by human foresight, was a thing unknown; but if he will only think, for a moment, of all the circumstances, consider the enormous velocity at which trains move, the tremendous strain thus thrown upon every portion of the road-bed and the machinery, I think the wonder will be why there are not more accidents. Think, for a moment, of one or two hundred tons' weight impelled through the air at a velocity of from one hundred to two hundred and forty feet per second, and tell me if you do not consider that the chances for damage are pretty numerous.

I remember once being detained at a way-station with the Up Express, waiting for the Down Express to pass me. We were both, owing to snow and ice on the rails, sadly behind time, and I had concluded just to wait where I was, until we heard from the other train, though a liberal construction of the rules gave me the right to proceed "with due caution;" but I was afraid that, if any thing *did* happen, there would be two opinions as to what "due caution" meant, so I held still. The passengers were all uneasy, as they always are, and stormed and fretted up and down, now coming to me and demanding, in just about such tones as we would imagine a newly caught she-bear to use, whether we intended "to keep them there all night?" whether I supposed "the traveling public would tamely submit to such outrages?" if I thought they "had no rights in the premises?" etc. These and similar questions were put to me, some peevishly, some in a lordly manner, evidently with the intention of bullying me into a start. I generally maintained the dirty but independent dignity of my position of "runner of that kettle;" but these latter Sir Oracles, I told that I was too well used to dealing with fire, water, steam and rock to be scared by a little "wind." After a while there came a telegraphic dispatch, unsigned, undated, but saying, "Come ahead;" this raised a terrible "hillabaloo." The passengers crowded into the cars and looked for an immediate start. The conductor came to me and said that he thought we had better start. I told him "No;" that I infinitely preferred to run on good solid rails rather than telegraph wires, at all times, and more especially when the wires brought such lame orders as these "Very well," says he, "I don't know but you are right, but I shall leave you to *console* these passengers—I'm off to hide," and away he went. Pretty soon out they came by twos, threes, dozens and scores; and I declare they needed consolation, for a madder set I never saw. Pshaw! talk about "hornets" and "bob-tailed bulls in fly-time;" they ain't a circumstance to a passenger on a railroad train which is an hour behind time. Well, they blustered and stormed, shook their fists at me, and about twenty took down my name with the murderous intent of "reporting" me at head-quarters, and "seeing about this thing" generally. At last some individual, bursting with wrath, called for an indignation meeting. The call was answered with alacrity. I attended as a disinterested spectator, of course; a President and Secretary were appointed, several speeches were made, overflowing with eloquence, and all aimed at me, but carrying a few shots for every body on the train, even to the boy that sold papers. This much had been done, and the committee on "resolutions which should be utterly annihilating," had just retired, when a whistle was heard up the track, and down came an extra engine, running as fast as she could, carrying no light, but bringing news that the " down train" was off the track eleven miles above, and bringing a requisition for all the doctors in town to care for the wounded, who were numerous. The " resolution committee" adjourned *sine die*. I was never reported, for they all saw that, had I done as they wished me to, I would have met this extra engine and rendered a few more doctors necessary for my own train. The blunder of the telegraph was never explained, but blunder it was, and the more firm was I never to obey a telegraphic dispatch without it was clear and distinct, " signed, sealed and delivered."

HUMAN LIVES vs. THE DOLLAR

HUMAN LIVES vs. THE DOLLAR.

CATTLE and horses on the track are a continual source of annoyance to engineers, and have been the occasion of many serious accidents. On the W. & S. Railroad, not many years since, an accident occurred, with the circumstances of which I was familiar, and which I will relate.

George Dean was one of the most accomplished and thorough engineers that I ever knew. He was running the Night Express, a fast run; while I was running the through freight, and met him at C—— station. I arrived there one night " on time," but George was considerably behind; so I had to wait for him. Just before George arrived at the station, he had to cross a bridge of about 200 feet span; it was a covered bridge, and the rails were some 30 feet from the water below.

I had been there waiting for him to pass, for over half an hour, when I heard his whistle sound at a "blind crossing" about a mile distant; so I knew he was coming; and as George was a pretty fast runner, I thought I would stand out on the track and see him come, as the track was straight, there, for nearly a mile.

I saw the glimmer of his head-light when he first turned the curve and entered upon the straight track, and pulled out my watch to time him to the station, through which he was to pass without stopping. The light grew brighter and brighter as he advanced with the speed of the wind, and he was within sixty feet of the bridge, when I saw an animal of some kind, I then knew not what it was, but it proved to be a horse, dart out on the track, right in front of the engine. George saw it, I know, for he gave the whistle for brakes, and a series of short puffs to scare the horse from the track; but it was of no use; the horse kept right on and ran towards the bridge. Arrived there, instead of turning to one side, it gave a jump right on to the bridge, and fell down between the ties, and there, of course, he hung. On came George's ponderous engine, and striking the horse, was thrown from the track into the floor timbers of the bridge, which gave way beneath the weight and the tremendous concussion, and down went the engine standing upon its front, the tender dropped in behind it, and the baggage car and one passenger car were heaped together on top of them both. I saw them drop, heard the crash, and at once, with the other men of my train, started to relieve any that might be caught in the wreck. Leaping down the embankment forming the approach of the bridge, I waded through the stream to where the engine stood, my fireman following close behind me. Looking up, we saw George caught on the head of the boiler. He was able to speak to us, and told us that he was not much hurt, but his legs were caught so that he could not move, and from the heat of the boiler he was literally roasting to death. We climbed up to where he was caught, to see if we could move him or get him out; but alas! he could not be helped. His legs lay right across the front of the boiler, and on them were resting some timbers of the broken baggage car, while the passenger car was so wedged into the bridge that there was no prospect of lifting it so as to get George out for many hours. I went and got him some water, and with it bathed his forehead and cooled his parching lips; he talking to me all the time and sending word to his wife and children. For a few minutes, he bore up under the pain most manfully; but at last, it grew too intolerable for any human being to bear, and George, than whom a braver soul never existed, shrieked and screamed in his agony. He begged and prayed to die. He entreated us to kill him, and put an end to his sufferings—he even cursed us for not doing it, asking us how we could stand and see him roast to death, knowing, too, as we did and he did, that he could not be saved. He begged for a knife to kill himself with, as he would rather die by his own hand at once than to linger in such protracted, awful agony. Oh! it was terrible, to stand there and see the convulsive twitchings of his muscles, to hear him pray for death, to watch him as his eyes set with pain, and hear his agonized entreaties for death any way, no matter how, so it was quick. At last it was ended, the horrible drama closed, and he died; but his shrieks will never die out from the memory of those who heard them. The next day, when we got him out, we found his legs were literally jammed to pieces and then baked to a cinder. The fireman we found caught between the trucks of the tender and the driving-wheel of the engine, and apparently not a bone left whole in his body; he was utterly smashed to pieces. You could not have told, only from his clothing, which hung in bloody fragments to his corpse, that he had ever been a human being. We got them out at last and buried them. Sadly and solemnly we followed them to the grave, and thought, with much dread, of when it would be our turn. They lie together, a plain stone marking their resting-place, and no railroad man ever visits their graves without a tear in tribute to their memory.

Thus they died, and thus all that knew them still mourn them. But the noise of the accident had scarcely ceased echoing amidst the adjoining hills, ere the owner of the horse was on the ground wishing to know if any one was there who was authorized to pay for his horse; this, too, in the face of the fact, afterward proven, that he himself had turned the horse upon the track, there to filch the feed.

FORTY-TWO MILES PER HOUR.

9

FORTY-TWO MILES PER HOUR.

NEARLY every person that we hear speak of travel by rail, thinks that he has, on numerous occasions, traveled at the rate of sixty miles an hour; but among engineers this is known to be an extremely rare occurrence. I myself have run some pretty fast machines, and never had much fear as to "letting them out," and I never attained that speed for more than a mile or two on a down grade, and with a light train, excepting on one or two occasions. Supposing, however, reader, that we look a little into what an engine has to do in order to run a mile in a minute, or more time. Say we go down to the depot, and take a ride on this Morning Express, which goes to Columbus in one hour and thirty-five minutes, making two stops. We will get aboard of the Deshler, one of the smartest engines on the road, originally built by Moore & Richardson, but since then thoroughly overhauled, and in fact rejuvenated, by that prince of *master*-mechanics, "Dick Bromley." And you may be sure she is in good trim for good work, as it is a habit with Dick to have his engines all so. She is run by that little fellow you see there, always looking good-natured, but getting around his engine pretty fast. That is "Johnny Andrews," and you can warrant that if Dick Bromley builds an engine, and Johnny runs her, and you ride behind her, you will have a pretty fast ride if the time demands it. The train is seven minutes behind time to-day, reducing the time to Columbus—55 miles—to one hour and twenty-eight minutes, and that with this heavy train of ten cars, all fully loaded. After deducting nine minutes more, that will undoubtedly be lost in making two stops, this will demand a speed of forty-two miles per hour; which I rather guess will satisfy you. You see the tender is piled full of wood, enough to last your kitchen fire for quite a while; but that has got to be filled again; for, ere we reach Columbus, we shall need two cords and a half. Look into the tank; you see it is full of water; but we shall have to take some more; for between here and Columbus, 1558 gallons of water must be flashed into steam, and sent traveling through the cylinders.

But we are off; you see this hill is before us; and looking behind, you will see that another engine is helping us. Notwithstanding that help, let us see what the Deshler is doing, and how Johnny manages her. She is carrying a head of steam which exerts on every square inch of the internal surface of the boiler, a pressure of 120 pounds. Take a glance at the size of the boiler; it is 17 feet 6 inches long, and 40 inches in diameter. Inside of it there is the fire-box, 48 inches long, 62 inches deep, and 36 across. From this to the front of the engine, you see a lot of flues running. There are 112 of these, 10 feet 6 inches long, and two inches in diameter; and of the inner surface of all this, every square inch is subjected to the aforesaid pressure, which amounts to a pressure of 95,005 pounds on each flue. Don't you think, if there is a weak place anywhere in this boiler, it will be mighty apt to give out? And if it does, and this enormous power is let loose at once, where will you and I go to? Don't be afraid, though; for *this* boiler is built strongly; every plate is right and sound. Open that fire-door. Do you hear that enormously loud cough? That is the noise made by the escape, through an opening of 31 square inches only, of the steam which has been at work in the cylinder. You can feel how it shakes the whole engine. And see how it stirs up the fire. Whew! isn't that rather a hot-looking hole? The heat there is about 2800° Centigrade scale. But we begin to go faster. Listen! try if you can count the sounds made by the escaping steam, which we call the "exhaust." No, you cannot; but at every one of those sounds, two solid feet of steam has been taken from the boilers, used in the cylinder, where it exerted on the piston, which is fourteen inches in diameter, a pressure of nine tons, and then let out into the air, making, in so doing, that noise. There are four of those "exhausts" to every revolution of the driving-wheels, during which revolution we advance only $17\frac{2}{3}$ feet. Now we are up to our speed, making 208 revolutions, changing $33\frac{1}{3}$ gallons of water into steam every minute we run, and burning eight solid feet of wood.

We are now running a mile in one minute and twenty-six seconds; the driving-wheels are revolving a little more than $3\frac{1}{2}$ times in each second; and steam is admitted into, and escapes from, the cylinders fifteen times in a second, exerting each time a force of nearly nine tons on the pistons. We advance 61 feet per second. Our engine weighs 22 tons; our tender about 17 tons; and each car in the train with passengers, about 17 tons; so that our whole train weighs, at a rough calculation, 209 tons, and should we strike an object sufficiently heavy to resist us, we would exert upon it a momentum of 12,749 tons—a force hard to resist!

Look out at the driving-wheels; see how swiftly they revolve. Those parallel rods, that connect the drivers, each weighing nearly 150 pounds, are slung around at the rate of 210 times a minute. Don't you think that enough is required of an engine to run 42 miles per hour, without making it gain 18 miles in that time? Those tender-wheels, too, have been turning pretty lively meanwhile— no less than 600 times per minute. Each piston has, in each minute we have traveled, moved about 700 feet. So you see that, all around, we have traveled pretty fast, and here we are in Columbus, "on time;" and I take it you are satisfied with 42 miles per hour, and will never hereafter ask for 60.

Let us sum up, and then bid good-bye to the Deshler and her accommodating runner, Johnny Andrews. The drivers have revolved 16,830 times. Steam has entered and been ejected from the cylinders 67,320 times. Each piston has traveled 47,766 feet, and we have run only 55 miles, at the rate of 42 miles per hour.

USED UP AT LAST.

USED UP AT LAST.

THE old proverb, that "the pitcher which goes often to the well returns broken at last," receives, in the lives of railroad men, frequent confirmation. I have known some men who have run engines for fifteen or twenty years and met with no accident worthy of note to themselves, their trains, or to any of the passengers under their charge; but if they continue running, the iron hand of fate will surely reach them.

Old Stephen Hanford, or "Old Steve," as he is called by everybody who knows him, had been running engines for twenty-five years, with an exemption from the calamities, the smash-ups and break-downs, collisions, etc., that usually checker the life of an engineer, that was considered by everybody most remarkable. Night and day,

in rain, snow and mist, he has driven his engine on over
flood and field, and landed his passengers safely at their
journey's end, always. No matter how hard the storm
blew, with sharp forked lightnings, with muttering thunders, and the pitiless, driving rain, Old Steve's engine,
which from its belching smoke and eating fire seemed the
demon of the storm, came in safe, and the old man, whose
eye never faltered, whose vigil never relaxed, got off from
his engine, and after seeing it safely housed, went to his
home, not to dream of the terrors and miseries of collisions, of the shrieks and groans of victims whom his engine had trodden down and crushed with tread as resist-
less as the rush of mountain torrents. No; all these saddening reflections were spared him, for he had never had
charge of an engine when any fatal accident happened.
Old Steve was one of the most careful men on an engine that I ever saw. He was always on the watch, and
was active as a cat. Nothing escaped his watchful glance,
and in any emergency his presence of mind never forsook
him; he went at once to doing the right thing, and did it
quickly.

The old man's activity never diminished in the least,
but his eyesight grew weak, and he thought he would leave

the main line, and, like an old war-horse, in his latter
days be rid of the hurry-skurry of the road. So he took
a switch engine in the yard at Rochester and worked there,
leaving the fast running in which he delighted to his
younger comrades, many of whom received their first in-
sight to the business from Old Steve. He had been
there about a year at work, very well contented with his
position, a little outside of the great whirling current of
the road on which he had so long labored, and was one
day standing beside his engine, almost as old a stager as
himself, when with an awful crash the boiler exploded.
Old Steve was not hurt by the explosion, but he started back so suddenly that he fell upon the other track, up
which another engine was backing; the engineer of
which, startled, no doubt, by the explosion, did not see
the old man, until too late, and the wheels passed over
him, crushing his leg off, just above the knee. They
picked him up and carried him home; "the pitcher had
been often to the well,"—it was broken at last. Owing
to his vigorous constitution, the shock did not kill him;
the leg was amputated, and now, should you ever be in the
depot at Rochester, you will most likely see Old Steve
there, hobbling around on one leg and a pair of crutches,

maimed, indeed, but as cheerful as ever. He said to me, "I am used up, but what right had I to expect any thing else? In twenty-five years I have bidden good-bye to many a comrade, who, in the same business, met the stern fate which will most surely catch us all if we stick to the . iron horse."

A VICTIM OF LOW WAGES.

A VICTIM OF LOW WAGES.

DURING an absence from home of several weeks, in the past summer, I traveled in safety, upwards of three thousand miles, but it was not because the danger was not there, not because the liabilities for accidents were not as great as ever; it was because human foresight did not happen to err, and nature happened to be propitious. The strength of her materials was as much tried as ever, but they were in condition to resist the strain; so I and my fellow passengers passed safely over many a place which awoke in me thrilling memories; for in one place, the gates of death had been in former time apparently swung wide to ingulf me, but I escaped; at another, I remember to have shut my eyes and held my breath, while my heart beat short and heavily, as the ponderous engine,

10 (145)

of which I had the control, crushed the bones and mangled the flesh of some poor wight caught upon the track, to save whom I had exercised every faculty I possessed, but all in vain; he was too near, and my train too heavy for me to stop in time to spare him. I met many of my old cronies during my absence, and, inquiring for others, heard the long-expected but saddening news, that they had gone; their running was over, the dangers they had so often faced overcame them at last, and now they sleep where " signal lights " and the shrill whistle denoting danger, which have so often called all their faculties into play to prevent destruction and save life, are no longer heard. Others I met, who, in some trying time, had been caught and crushed by the very engines they had so often held submissive to their will, and now, maimed and crippled, they must hobble along till the almost welcome voice of death bids them come and lay their bones beside their comrades in danger, who have gone before.

A little paragraph in the papers last winter, announced that a gravel train, of which Hartwell Stark was engineer, and James Burnham conductor, had collided with a freight train, on the N. Y. C. R. R.; that the fireman was killed, and the engineer so badly hurt that he was not expected to live. Perhaps a fuller account of this catastrophe may be instructive in order to show the risks run by railroad men, the responsibility resting upon the most humble of them, and the enormous amount of suffering a man is capable of enduring and yet live. This gravel train " laid up " for the night at Clyde, and in the morning early, as soon as the freight trains bound west had passed, proceeded out upon the road to its work. It was the duty of the switchman to see that the trains had all passed, and report the same to the men in charge of the gravel train. This morning it was snowing very hard, the wind blew strong from the east, and take it altogether, it was a most unpleasant time, and one very likely to put all trains behind. Knowing this, the conductor and engineer both asked the switchman if the freights had all passed. He replied positively that they had. So, without hesitation, they proceeded to their work. They had left their train of gravel cars at a " gravel pit," some sixteen miles distant; so with the engine backing up and dragging the " caboose," in which were about thirty men, they started. They had got about ten miles on their way, the wind and snow still blowing in their faces, rendering it almost impossible for them to see any thing ahead, even in daylight—utterly so in the darkness of that morning, just before day—when, out of the driving storm, looking a very demon of destruction, came thundering on at highest speed, the freight train, which the switchman had so confidently reported as having passed an hour before they left Clyde. The engineer of the freight train jumped, and said that before he struck the ground he heard the collision. Hart tried to reverse his engine, but had not time to do it; so he could not jump, but was caught in the close embrace of those huge monsters. The freight engine pushed the "tender" of his engine up on to the "foot-board." It divided; one part crushed the fireman up against the dome and broke in the "fire-door;" the wood piled over on top of him, and the flames rushing out of the broken door soon set it on fire, and there he lay till he was taken out, eighteen hours afterward, a shapeless cinder of humanity. The other part caught Hart's hips between it and the "run-board," and rolled him around for about six feet, breaking both thigh-bones; and to add to his sufferings a piece of the "hand-rail" was thrust clear through the flesh of both legs, and twisted about there till it made gashes six inches long. The steam pipe being broken off, the hissing steam prevented his feeble cries from being heard, and as every man in the "caboose" was hurt, Hart began to think that iron rack of misery must surely be his death-bed. At last, however, some men saw him, but at first they were afraid to come near, being fearful of an explosion of the boiler. Soon, however, some more bold than the rest went to work, and procuring a T rail, they proceeded to pry the wreck apart, and release him from his horrible position. And so, after being thus suspended and crushed for over half an hour, he was taken down, put upon a hand-car, and taken to his home at Clyde, which place he reached in five hours after the accident. No one expected him to live. The physicians were for an immediate amputation of both limbs, but to this Hart stoutly objected. So they finally agreed to wait forty-eight hours and see. At the end of that time—owing to his strong constitution and temperate habits of life—the inflammation was so light they concluded to leave poor Hart with both his legs, and there he has lain ever since. For twelve weeks he was never moved from his position in the bed, his clothes were never changed, and he never stirred so much as an inch; and even to this day—May 20th—he is unable to turn in the bed, though he can sit up, and when I saw him, was sitting in the stoop cutting potatoes for planting, and apparently as happy as a child, to think he could once more snuff fresh air.

I should think that such accidents (and they are of frequent occurrence) would teach the managers of railroads that the policy of hiring men who can be hired for twenty-five dollars a month, and who have so little judgment as to sleep on their posts, and then make such reports as this switchman did, endangering not only the property of the company, but also jeopardizing the lives of brave and true men like Hart Stark, and subjecting them to these lingering tortures, is suicidal to their best interests. Would not an extra ten dollars a month to all switchmen be a good investment, if in the course of a year it saved the life of one poor fireman, who otherwise would die as this poor fellow did; or if it saved one cool and true man from the sufferings Hart Stark has for the past five months endured?

CORONERS' JURIES vs. RAILROAD MEN

CORONERS' JURIES vs. RAILROAD MEN.

CORONER's juries are, beyond a doubt, a very good institution, and were established for a good purpose ; they investigate sudden deaths, while the matter is still fresh, before the cause has become hidden or obscured by lapse of time, and in most cases they undoubtedly arrive at a just conclusion ; but in cases of railroad accidents, I never yet knew one that was not unjust, to a greater or less degree, in its verdict against employees of the company on the train at the immediate time of the occurrence.

I know that in saying this I fly into the face of all the newspapers of the land, for they have a stereotyped sneer in these words, " *Of course* nobody was to blame," at every coroner's jury that fails to censure somebody, or to adjudge some one guilty of wilful murder.   Nevertheless I believe

it, and unhesitatingly declare it.   Most generally it is the
engineer and conductor who are censured, sometimes the
brakemen or switchmen; but rarely or never is it the right
one who is branded and placed in the newspaper pillory
as unfit to occupy any position of trust, and guilty of the
death of those killed and the wounds of those wounded.
As to an accident that could not be avoided by human
forethought, that idea is scouted, and if a coroner's jury
does ever so far forget what is expected of it by these edi-
tors—who are the self-elected bull-dogs of society, and
must needs bark or lose their dignity—why no words are
sufficiently sarcastic, no sentences sufficiently bitter, to
express the contempt which they feel for that benighted
coroner's jury.   To be sure they know nothing, or next
to nothing, of the circumstances, and the jury knows *all*
about them.   To be sure, iron will break and so will wood;
the insidious frost will creep in where man cannot probe,
and render as brittle as glass what should be tough as
steel; watches will go wrong, and no hundred men can be
found who will on all occasions give one interpretation to
the same words.   But what of that?

Why, the bare idea that any accident upon any road
can happen, and some poor devil of an engineer, con-

ductor, brakeman or switchman not be ready at hand, to be made into a pack-horse on whom to pile all the accumulated bile of these men who, many of them, have some private grudge to satisfy—the idea, I say, is preposterous to these men, and they fulminate their thunders against railroad men, until community gets into the belief that virtue, honesty, integrity or common dog sense are things of which a railroad man must necessarily be entirely destitute; and they are looked upon with distrust, they are driven to become clannish, and frequently, I must confess, any thing but polite to the traveling public, whose only greeting to them is gruff fault-finding, or an incessant string of foolish questions. But are they so much to blame for this? Would you, my reader, "cast your pearls before swine?" and can you particularly blame men for not being over warm to the traveling community which almost invariably treats them as machines, destitute of feeling, for whose use it pays so much a mile? Railroad men, though, are not impolite, nor short to everybody. Ask a jovial, good-natured man, who has a smile and a pleasant word for everybody, and I'll warrant he will tell you that he gets treated well enough on railroads; that the engineer answers his questions readily; that the

brakeman sees that he has a seat; that his baggage is
not bursted open every trip he takes, and the conductor
does not wake him up out of his sleep every five minutes
to ask for his ticket.   But ask a pursy, lordly individual,
whose lack of brains is atoned for by the capacity of his
stomach, who never asks for any thing, always orders it,
and who always praises the last road he was on, and d—s
the one he is now on; or ask a vinegar-looking, hatchet-
faced old maid, who has eight bandboxes, a parasol, an um-
brella, a loose pair of gloves, a work-bag and a poodle dog,
who always has either such a cold that she knows she
"shall die unless that window in front is put down," or
else is certain that she "shall suffocate unless more air is
let into the car," and who is continually asking whoever
she sees with a badge on, whether the "biler is going to
bust," or if "that last station ain't the one she bought
her ticket for?"—ask either of these (and there are a
great many travelers who, should they see this, would declare that I meant to be personal), and they will tell you
that railroad men are "rascals, sir! scamps, sir! every
one of them, sir!   Why, only the other day I had a bran-
new trunk, and I particularly cautioned the baggageman
and conductor to be careful, and would you believe it,

sir? when I got it, two—yes, sir! two—of the brass nails were jammed. Railroad men, from the dirty engineer to the stuck-up conductor, are bent on making the public as uncomfortable as they can, sir!" Reader, take my advice, and when you want any thing, go to the proper person and politely ask for it, and you will get it; but don't jump off and ask the engineer at every station how far it is to the next station? and how fast he ever did run? and if he ever knew John Smith of the Pontiac, and Buckwheat of the Sangamon and Pollywog road, one or the other, but really you forget which; but no matter, he must know him, for he looked so and so. Take care; while you are describing the venerable John Smith, that long oil-can may give an ugly flirt, and your wife have good cause for grumbling at your greasy cassimere inexpressibles; or a wink from the engineer to his funny fireman, may open that "pet cock," and your face get washed with rather nasty feeling water, and the shock might not be good for you. Don't bore the conductor with too many questions. If you ask civil questions, he will civilly answer you; but if you bore him too much by asking how fast "this ingine can run?" he may get cross, or he may tell how astonishingly fast the celebrated and

mythical Thomas Pepper used to run the equally celebrated and mythical locomotive, "Blowhard." I started
this article to tell a story illustrating my opinion of coroners' juries, but have turned it into a sort of homily on
the grievances of railroad men. No matter; the story
will keep, and the traveling people deserve a little talking
to about the way they treat railroad men.

ADVENTURES

OF

AN IRISH RAILROAD MAN.

ADVENTURES OF AN IRISH RAILROAD MAN.

On a railroad, as everywhere else, one meets with de-
cidedly "rich" characters—those whose every act is
mirth-provoking, and who, as the Irishman said, "can't
open their mouths without putting their fut in it." Such
an one was Billy Brown, who has been, for nearly thirteen
years, a brakeman on one road; who has run through and
escaped many dangers; who has seen many an old comrade depart this life for—let us hope, a better one.
Scarce an accident has happened on the road in whose
employ he has been so long, but Billy has somehow been
there; and always has Billy been kind to his dying
friends. Many a one of them has breathed out his last
sigh in Billy's ear; and I have often heard him crooning
out some wild Irish laments (for Billy is a full-blooded

11

Patlander), as he held in his lap the head of some of his comrades whose life was fast ebbing away from a mangled limb. I well remember one time, when one of Billy's particular cronies, Mike—the other name has escaped my memory—was missing from the train to which he was attached. A telegraphic dispatch was sent to the last station to see if he was left there; but, no! he was seen to get aboard the train as it left the station. So the conclusion was clear that Mike had fallen off somewhere on the road. Half a dozen of us, Billy with the rest, jumped into a hand-car, and went back to find him. We went once over the road without seeing any thing; but, as we came back, on passing the signboard which said " 80 rods to the drawbridge," we saw some blood on it; and, on looking down under the trestlework, we saw poor Mike's body lying half in the water and half on the rocks. It was but an instant ere we were down there; but the first look convinced us that he was dead. As the train was passing over the bridge, he had incautiously put out his head to look ahead, and it had come in contact with the signboard, and was literally smashed flat. No sooner had the full conviction that Mike was dead taken possession of Billy, than he whops down on his knees, and commences kissing the fellow's bloody face, at the same time, with many tears, apostrophizing his body somewhat after this fashion: " Oh! wirra, wirra, Mike dear! Mike dear! and is this the way ye're afther dyin' to git yer bloody ould hed smashed in wid a dirty old guideboord ? "

We all felt sad, and sympathized fully with Billy's grief; but the ludicrousness with which he expressed it, was too much for any of us; and we turned away, not to hide a tear, but to suppress a smile, and choke down a laugh.

But Billy was very clannish ; and, to use his own expression, " the passenger might go hang, if there was any of the railroad byes in the muss." But as soon as Billy's fears as to any of his comrades being injured were allayed, no man could be more efficient than he in giving aid to anybody. Billy was true to duty, and never forgot what to do, if it was only in the usual routine of his business. Outside of that, however, he could commit as many Irish bulls as any one.

I well remember one night I had the night freight to haul. We were going along pretty good jog, when the bell rang for me to stop. I stopped and looked back to see what could be the matter. I saw no stir; so after

waiting awhile, I started back to see if I could find any
one. After getting back about twenty cars, I found that
the train was broken in two, and that the rest of the cars
were away back out of sight. I hallooed to my fireman
to bring a light, and started on foot back around the
curve, to see where they were. I got to the curve, and
saw a light coming up the track towards me; the man
who carried it was evidently running as fast as he could.
I stopped to see who it was; and in a few moments he
approached near enough to hail me—when, mistaking me
for a trackman, and without slackening his speed the
least, Billy Brown—for it was he—bellowed out, with a
voice like a stentor, only broken by his grampus-like
blowing, " I say, I say, did yees see iver innything of a
train goin' for Albany like h—l jist now ? " I believe I
never did laugh quite so heartily in my life, as I did then;
and Billy, turning around, addressed me in the most ag-
grieved manner possible, saying : " Pon me sowl now,
Shanghi, its mighty mane of yees to be scarin' the life out
of me wid that laff of yours, an' I strivin' as hard as iver
I could to catch up wid yees, and bring yees back, to take
the resht of yere train which ye were afther lavin in the
road a bit back."

Another adventure of Billy's, at which we liked to have killed ourselves with laughter, and Billy himself liked to have died from fright, occurred in this wise: I was taking the stock train down the road one very dark night, and Billy was one of the brakemen. Attached to the rear of the train were five empty emigrant cars, which we were hauling over the road. I was behind time, and was running about as fast as I could, to make up the lost time; when the bell rang for me to stop. I stopped; and going back to see what was the matter, I found that two of the emigrant cars had become detached from the train, and been switched off into the river, just there very close to the track and very deep; and there they lay, one of them clear out of sight, and the other cocked up at an angle of about 45 degrees, with one end sticking out of the water about six feet. On looking around, I found that all the men were there on hand, except Billy; and he was nowhere to be found. We at last concluded that he must have been in the cars that were thrown into the river, and was drowned. But in this we were soon shown our error; for, from the car that was sticking out of the water, came a confused sound of splashing, and praying, and swearing, which soon convinced us that Billy was at least not dead. We hallooed at him, and asked him if he was hurt. His answer was, "Divil a hurt, but right nigh drowned; an how'll I get out o' this?" We told him to get out of the door. "But it's locked." "Unlock it then." "Shure, frow me a kay an' I will." "Where is your own key?" "Divil a wan o' me knows. Gone drownded I ixpect." "How deep is the water where you are, Billy?" "Up till me chin, an' the tide a risin'. Oh! murther, byes, hilp me out o' this; for I'm kilt intirely wid the wet and the cowld and the shock til me syshtem——" But we told him we couldn't help him, and that he must crawl out of a window. "Howly Moses," says Billy, "an' don't ye know these is imigrant cars, an' the windows all barred across to kape thim fules from sticking out their heads? an' how'll I get out? Byes, byes, wad ye see me drown, an' I so close to land, an' in a car to bute? Ah! now cease yere bladgin, an' hilp me out o' this." After bothering him to our hearts' content, we got a plank, and crawled out to the car, only about ten feet from shore, and cutting a hole in the top, soon had Billy at liberty.

A BAD BRIDGE.

A BAD BRIDGE.

ONE cold winter's night, while I was running on the H—— Road, I was to take the Night Express down the road. The day had been excessively stormy; the snow had fallen from early dawn till dark, and blown and drifted so on the track, that all trains were behind time. Especially was this so on the upper end of the road; the lower end, over which I was to run, was not so badly blockaded; in fact, on the southern portion, the storm had been of rain. The train came in three hours behind, consisting of twenty cars, all heavily loaded with grumbling, discontented passengers. This was more of a train than I could handle with my engine, even on the best of rail; but where the rail was so slippery with snow or ice as it was that night, it was utterly impossible for me to do any thing with it.

(169)

So, orders were given for another engine to couple in with me; and George P——, with the Oneida, did so.

I was on the lead. George coupled in behind me. We both had fast "machines;" and in a little quiet talk we had before starting, we resolved to do some pretty fast running where we could.

The hungry passengers at last finished their meal, it being a refreshment station; the bell was rang; "all aboard" shouted; and we pulled out. Like twin brothers those engines seemed to work. Their "exhausts" were as one, and each with giant strength tugged at the train. We plowed through the snow, and it flew by us in fleecy, feathery flakes, on which our lights shone so bright that it seemed as if we were plunging into a cloud of silver dust. On! on! we rushed; the few stops we had to make were made quickly; and past the stations at which we were not to stop, we rushed thunderingly: a jar, a rumble, a shriek of the whistle, and the glimmering station-lights were away back out of sight.

At last we were within fourteen miles of the terminus of our journey. Both engines were doing their utmost, and the long train behind us was trailing swiftly on. Soon the tedious night-ride would be over; soon the weary limbs might rest. We were crossing a pile bridge in the middle of which was a draw. The rising of the water in the river had lifted the ice, which was frozen to the piles, and thus, I suppose, weakened the bridge, so that, when our two heavy engines struck it, it gave away. I was standing at my post, when, by the sudden strain and dropping of the engine, I knew that we were off the track, but had no idea of the real nature of the calamity. My engine struck her forward end upon the abutments of the bridge, knocking the forward trucks from under her. She held there but an instant of time; but in that instant I and my fireman sprang upon the runboard, and from thence to the solid earth. We turned in time to see the two engines go down into the water, there thirty feet deep; and upon them were piled the baggage, mail and express cars, while the passenger cars were some thrown from the track on one side, some on the other. The terrible noise made by the collision and the hissing made by the cold waters wrapping the two engines in their chill embrace, deafened and appalled us for an instant; but the next, we were running back to help the wounded. We found many wounded and seven dead amidst the wreck of the cars; but seven more were missing, and among them were six of the railroad men. After searching high and low, amidst the portion of the wreck on dry land, we with one accord looked shudderingly down into those black, chilling waters, and knew that there they lay dead. All night long we sat there. The wild wintry blasts howled around us ; the cold waters gurgled and splashed amid the wreck ; we could hear the wounded groan in their pains ; but we listened in vain for the voices we were wont to hear. The chill tide, over which the ice was even then congealing anew, covered them. Mayhap they were mangled in the collision, and their shriek of pain was hushed and drowned as the icy waters rippled in over their lips. We almost fancied, when we threw the light of our lanterns upon the black flood, that we could see their white faces turned up toward us, frozen into a stony, immovable look of direst fear and agonizing entreaty.

Morning came, and still we could not reach our friends and comrades. Days went by before they were found, but when found each man was at his post. None had jumped or flinched, all went down with the wreck, and were found jammed in ; but their countenances wore no look of fear, the icy waters that congealed their expression, did not find a coward's look among them ; all wore a stern, unflinching expression that would have shown you, had you seen them just ere they went down, that they would do as they did do, stick bravely to their posts, and go down with the wreck, doing their duty at the cost of their lives.

A WARNING.

A WARNING.

I AM not, nor was I ever, superstitious. I do not believe in dreams, signs, witches, hobgoblins, nor in any of the rest of that ilk with which antiquated maidens were in olden time used to cheer the drooping spirits of childhood, and send us urchins off to our bed, half scared to death, expecting to see some horrid monster step out from every corner of the room, and in unearthly accents declare his intention to " grind our bones for coffee," or do something else equally horrid, the contemplation of which was in an equal degree unfitted to render our sleep sound or our rest placid. Somehow the visitors from the other world, that children used to be told of, were never pretty nor angelic, but always more devilish than any thing else. But in these days, this has changed; for the ghosts

12 (177)

in which gullible people deal now, are preëminently silly things. They use their superhuman strength in tumbling parlor furniture about the rooms, and in drumming on the floors and ceilings of bed-rooms. The old proverb is, that " every generation grows weaker and wiser." In this respect, however, we have reversed the proverb ; for a great many have grown stronger in gullibility and weaker in intellect, else we would not have so many spiritualists who wait for God and His angels to thump out their special revelations, or else tumble a table about the room to the tune of A B C.

I have known, as have many, probably all of my readers, a great many people who professed to have the firmest faith in dreams and signs, who were always preadmonished of every event by some supernatural means, and who invariably are looking out for singular events when they have been visited by a singular dream. I have never believed in these things, have always laughed at them, and do so still. Yet there is one circumstance of my life, of this kind, that is shrouded in mystery, that I cannot explain, that I know to be so, and yet can scarcely believe, when a warning was given to me somehow, I know not how, that shook me and influenced me, despite my ridi-

cule of superstition and disbelief in signs or warnings of
any kind; so that I heeded it, and, by so doing, saved
myself from instant death, and saved also many passengers who, had they known of the " warning" which influenced me to take the steps which I did, would have
laughed at me, and endeavored to drive me on. The
facts are briefly as follows—I tell them, not attempting to
explain them, nor offering any theory concerning them—
neither pretending that angels or devils warned me, and
only knowing that it was so:

I was running a Night Express train, and had a train
of ten cars—eight passenger and two baggage cars—and
all were well loaded. I was behind time, and was very
anxious to make a certain point; therefore I was using
every exertion, and putting the engine to the utmost
speed of which she was capable. I was on a section of
the road usually considered the best running ground on
the line, and was endeavoring to make the most of it,
when a conviction struck me that I must stop. A something seemed to tell me that to go ahead was dangerous,
and that I must stop if I would save life. I looked back
at my train, and it was all right. I strained my eyes
and peered into the darkness, and could see no signal of

danger, nor any thing betokening danger, and there I
could see five miles in the daytime. I listened to the
working of my engine, tried the water, looked at the
scales, and all was right. I tried to laugh myself out of
what I then considered a childish fear; but, like Banquo's
ghost, it would not down at my bidding, but grew stronger
in its hold upon me. I thought of the ridicule I would
have heaped upon me, if I did stop; but it was all of no
avail. The conviction—for by this time it had ripened
into a conviction—that I must stop, grew stronger, and I
resolved to stop; and I shut off, and blew the whistle for
brakes, accordingly. I came to a dead halt, got off, and
went ahead a little way, without saying any thing to anybody what was the matter. I had my lamp in my hand,
and had gone about sixty feet, when I saw what convinced me that premonitions are sometimes possible. I dropped the lantern from my nerveless grasp, and sat down on
the track, utterly unable to stand; for there was a switch,
the thought of which had never entered my mind, as it
had never been used since I had been on the road, and
was known to be spiked, but which now was open to lead
me off the track. This switch led into a stone quarry,
from whence stone for bridge purposes had been quarried,

and the switch was left there, in case stone should be needed at any time; but it was always kept locked, and the switch-rail spiked. Yet here it was, wide open; and, had I not obeyed my preadmonition—warning—call it what you will—I should have run into it, and, at the end of the track, only about ten rods long, my heavy engine and train, moving at the rate of forty-five miles per hour, would have come into collision with a solid wall of rock, eighteen feet high. The consequences, had I done so, can neither be imagined nor described; but they could, by no possibility, have been otherwise than fatally horrid.

This is my experience in getting warnings from a source that I know not and cannot divine. It is a mystery to me—a mystery for which I am very thankful, however, although I dare not attempt to explain it, nor say whence it came.

SINGULAR ACCIDENTS.

SINGULAR ACCIDENTS.

THE brothers G. are well known to all travelers by the route of the N. Y. C. R. R. They have been a long time employed there, and by the traveling public and the company that employ them they are universally esteemed; but the star of them all, the one most loved by his companions in toil, respected by travelers, and trusted by his employers, was Thomas, who met with his death in one of those calamitous accidents which so frequently mar the career of the railroad man. I was an eye-witness of the accident, and shall attempt to describe it.

The day on which it occurred was a glorious summer one; the breeze wafted a thousand pleasant odors to my senses; the birds sang their sweetest songs. As I was journeying along the highway between Weedsport and

Jordan, I heard the rumble of the approaching train, and as from where I was I could get a fair view of the passing train, which was the fastest on the road and was behind time a few minutes, I stopped to watch it as it passed. On it came, the sun glancing on the polished engine as it sped along like the wind. The track where I had stopped, was crossed by two roads, one of them crossing at right angles, the other diagonally; between the two crossings there was a large pile of ties placed, probably eight feet from the track. I saw the engine, which was running at full speed, pass the pile, when suddenly, without warning, in a second of time, the cars went piling and crashing over the bank into a promiscuous heap, crushed into each other like eggshells. One of them, a full-sized car, turned a complete somersault; another was turned once and a half around, and lay with one end down in the ditch, and the other up to the track, while the third went crashing into its side. I hitched my horse and ran over to the scene, expecting, of course, that not a soul would be found alive; arrived there, I found that no person was killed but poor Tom, and not over a dozen hurt, although the cars were crowded, and not a seat was left whole in the cars, which were perfectly riddled. They had already found Tom's body, which lay under the truck of the first passenger car, which had been torn out, and one wheel lay on his neck. He had no need of care, no need of sympathy, for the first crash killed him; and so with no notice, no warning, no moment for a faintly whispered good-bye to those he loved, poor Tom passed away to the unknown shore, leaving many friends to grieve for him.

We got him out, laid him beside the track, and stood solemnly by; grieving that he, our friend, had gone and left no message for the wife who idolized him, the brothers who had loved him, or the friends who so fully appreciated his many noble qualities. While we stood thus speechless with heartfelt, choking grief, a man came up and asked for the man who had charge of the train. Some one, I forget who, pointed to the mangled form of poor Tom and said, "There is all that is mortal of him." Said the thing —I will not call him man—"Dear me! I'm sorry; I wanted to find some one to pay for my cow."

It was his cow that had caused the accident, by jumping out against the baggage car after the engine had passed.

Another singular accident occurred on a road in the State of New York. An engine, to which something had happened that required a couple of sticks of wood out on the run-board as fulcrum for a lever, was passing through a station at full speed, when one of the sticks, that had carelessly been left outside, fell off and was struck by the end of the main rod on the backward stroke ; impelled backwards by the force of the blow, it struck a man, standing carelessly beside the track, full on the side of the head, fracturing his skull, and killing him instantly.

LUDICROUS INCIDENTS.

LUDICROUS INCIDENTS.

THERE is not often much that is comic on the " rail," but occasionally an incident occurs that brings a loud guffaw from everybody who witnesses it.

I remember once standing by the side of an engine that was switching in the yard. The fellow who was running it I thought, from his actions while oiling, was drunk, so I watched him. He finished oiling, and clambered up on to the foot-board and attempted, in obedience to the orders of the yard-man, to start out. He jerked and jerked at the throttle-lever, but all to no effect; the engine would not budge an inch. I saw from where I stood what was the matter, and although nearly bursting with laughter, I refrained from telling him, but looked on to see the fun. After pulling for at least a dozen times, he bawled out to the yard-man that he couldn't go, and then gave another twitch, but it was of no use ; then he stepped back a step or two and looked at the throttle, with a look of the most stupid amazement that I ever saw ; his face expressed the meaning of the word "dumbfoundered" completely.　At last the fireman showed him what was the matter.　It was simply that he had set the thumb-screw on the throttle-lever and neglected to unloose it, in each of his efforts.

Another laughable affair occurred on one of the Eastern roads, I forget which.　An engine stood on the switch, all fired up and ready to start ; the hands were all absent at dinner.　A big black negro, who was loafing around the yard, became exceedingly inquisitive as to how the thing was managed—so up he gets and began to poke around. He threw the engine into the forward gear and gave it steam, of course not knowing what he was doing ; but of that fact the engine was ignorant, and at once, like a mettled steed, it sprung to full speed and away it went, carrying the poor darkey an unwilling dead-head ride.　He did not know how to stop it, and dare not jump, for, as he himself expressed it, when found, " Gorra mity, she mos flew." The engine of course ran until steam ran down, which was not in fourteen miles, and Mr. Darkey got off and put for the woods. He didn't appear at that station again for over a week. He said that "ef de durn ting had a gon much furder he guessed he'd a bin white folks."

"Ol Long," an old friend of mine, tells a pretty good story about an old white horse that he struck once. Ol says that he was running at about thirty miles an hour, when an old white horse jumped out on the track right in front of the engine, which struck him and knocked him away down into the ditch, where he lay heels up. He of course expected that the horse was killed, and so reported on arriving at the end of the road ; but what was his surprise, on returning the next day, to see the self-same old nag quietly eating by the side of the road. Ol says he believes the old fellow did look rather sour at him, but he could not apologize.

13

EXPLOSIONS.

EXPLOSIONS

IT is easy to account for explosions of boilers on the hypothesis of too great pressure; but it is hardly ever very easy—frequently utterly impossible—to account for the causes which induce that overpressure. There are, to be sure, a number of reasons which may be advanced. The engineer may have screwed the scales down too much, and thus, the safety-valve not operating to let off the surplus steam, a force may be generated within the boiler of such tremendous power that the strong iron will be rent and torn like tissue-paper. This I say may occur, but in my experience I never knew of such a case. Then again, the water may get so low in the boiler that, on starting the engine and injecting cold water upon the hot plates, steam will be generated so suddenly as not to find vent, and in such enormous quantities and of so high a temperature as to explode the strongest boiler. Again, the water may be allowed to get low in the boiler, and the plates getting extremely hot, the motion of the train would generate steam enough by splashing water against them to cause an explosion. A proper care and due attention to the gauges would obviate this, and render explosion from these causes impossible. A piece of weak or defective iron, too, may have been put into the boiler at the time of its manufacture, and go on apparently safe for a long time, until at last it gives way under precisely the same pressure of steam that it has all along held with safety, or it may be with even less than it has often carried. How the engineer is to obviate this most fruitful cause of explosions, for the life of me I cannot see; still if his engine does blow up, everybody and their wives will believe that it happened entirely through his neglect. A person who has never seen an explosion, can form no idea of the enormous power with which the iron is rent. I saw one engine that had exploded, at a time too when, according to the oaths of three men, it had a sufficiency of water and only 95 lbs. of steam to the square inch, and was moving at only an ordinary speed, yet it was blown 65 feet from the track, and the whole of one side, from the " check joint" back to the " cab," was torn wide open—the lower portion hanging down to the ground, folded over like a table-leaf, and the other portion lay clear over to the other side, while from the rent, the jagged ends of more than half of the flues projected, twisted into innumerable shapes. The frame on that side was broken, and the ends stuck out from the side at right angles with their former position. I saw another, where the whole boiler front was blown out and the engine tipped clear over backwards on to the tender and freight car, where the engineer and fireman were found, crushed into shapeless masses, lying in the midst of the wreck. The engine Manchester exploded while standing at a station on the H. R. R. R., and killed two out of five men, who were standing together beside the tender. Two of those who were left, deposed, on oath, that not three minutes before the accident occurred, the engineer tried the water and found fully three gauges, while there was a pressure of only ninety-five pounds to the square inch, and it was blowing off.

How to account for it no one could tell, so every one who knew any thing whatever in regard to such things, called it " another of the mysterious visitations of God."

But the newspapers called it an evidence of gross care-lessness on the part of the engineer.

Several explosions have been known where the upper tubes were found unhurt, while the lower ones were, some of them, found badly burnt. The conclusion in these cases was that the tubes were too close together, and the water was driven away from them; consequently the start-ing of the engine, or the pumping of cold water into the boiler, was sufficient to cause an explosion.

HOW A FRIEND WAS KILLED.

HOW A FRIEND WAS KILLED.

————

THERE is among the remembrances of my life as a railroad man, one of such sadness, that I never think of it without a sigh. Every man, unless he be so morose that he cannot keep a dog, has his particular friends; those in whom he confides, and to whom he is always cheerful; whose society he delights in, and the possibility of whose death, he will never allow himself to admit.

Such a friend had I in George II——. We were inseparable—both of us unmarried; we would always manage to board together, and on all possible occasions to be together. Did George's engine lay up for the Sunday at one end of the road, and mine at the other, one of us was sure to go over the road "extra," in order that we might be together.

(203)

George and I differed in many respects, but more especially in this, that whereas I was one of the "fast" school of runners, who are never so contented with running as when mounted on a fast engine, with an express train, and it behind time.   George preferred a slow train, where, as he said, his occupation was "killing time," not "making" it.   So while I had the "Baltic," a fast engine, with drivers six feet and a half in diameter, and usually ran express trains, George had the "Essex," a freight engine, with four feet drivers.

One Saturday night I took the last run north, and was to "lay over" with my engine for the Sunday at the northern terminus of the road, until two o'clock Monday P. M.   George had to run the "Night Freight" down that night, and as we wished particularly to be together the next day, I concluded to go "down the line" with him.   Starting time came, and off we started.   I rode for awhile in the "caboose," as the passenger car attached to a freight train is called, but as the night was warm and balmy, the moon shining brightly, tinging with silvery white the great fleecy clouds that swept through the heaven, like monstrous floating islands of snow drifting over the fathomless waters of the sea, I went out and rode with George on the engine. The night was indeed most beautiful, the moonlight shimmering across the river, which the wind disturbed and broke into many ripples, made it to glow and shine like a sea of molten silver. The trees beside the track waved and beckoned their leafy tops, looking sombre and weird in the half-darkness of the night. The vessels we saw upon the river, gliding before the freshening breeze, with their signal lights glimmering dimly, and the occasional steamers with light streaming from every window, and the red light of their fires casting an unearthly glare upon the waters; these all combined to make the scene spread before us, as we rushed shrieking and howling over the road, one of unexcelled beauty. We both gazed at it, and said that if all scenes in the life of a railroad man were as beautiful as this we would wish no other life.

But something ailed George's engine. Her pumps would not work. After tinkering with them awhile, he asked the fireman if there was plenty of water in the tank; the fireman said there was, but to make assurance doubly sure I went and looked, and lo! there was not a drop! Before passing through the station George had asked the fireman if there was plenty of water. He replied that there was ; so George had run through the station, it not being a regular stopping place for the train, and here we were in a fix.   George thought he could run from where we had stopped to the next water station ; so he cut loose from the train and started.   We had stopped on the outside of a long curve, to the other end of which we could see ; it was fully a half mile, but the view was straight across the water—a bay of the river sweeping in there, around which the track went.

In about twenty minutes after George had left we saw him coming around the farthest point of the curve ; the brakeman at once took his station with his light at the end of the cars, to show George precisely where the train stood.   The engine came swiftly towards us, and I soon saw he was getting so near that he could not stop without a collision, unless he reversed his engine at once ; so I snatched the lamp from out the brakeman's hands, and swung it wildly across the track, but it was of no avail. On came the engine, not slackening her speed the least. We saw somebody jump from the fireman's side, and in the instant of time allowed us, we looked to see George jump, but no ! he stuck to his post, and there came a shock as of a mountain falling.   The heavy freight engine running, as it was, at as high a rate of speed as it could make, crashed into the train; thirteen cars were piled into a mass of ruins, the like of which is seldom seen.   The tender was turned bottom side up, with the engine lying atop of it, on its side.   The escaping steam shrieked and howled; the water, pouring in on to the fire, crackled and hissed; the stock (sheep and cattle) that were in the cars bellowed and bleated in their agony, and it seemed as if all the legions of hell were there striving to make a pandemonium of that quiet place by the river-side.   As soon as we recovered from the shock and got used to the din which at first struck terror to our hearts—and I think no sound can be more terrible than the bellowing of a lot of cattle that are crushed in a railroad smash-up—we went to work to see if George was alive, and to get him out, dead or alive.   We found him under the tender, but one side of the tank lay across his body, so that he could not move. We got rails and lifted and pried, until we raised the tender and got him out.   We took one of the doors from the wrecked cars, laid it beside the track, and made a bed on it with our coats and the cushions from the caboose; for poor George said he wanted to pass the few moments left him of earth beneath the open sky, and with the cool

breeze to fan his cheek.   Of course we dispatched a man
to the nearest station for aid, and to telegraph from there
for an engine; but it was late at night, everybody was
asleep, and it was more than three hours before any one
arrived, and all that time George lingered, occasionally
whispering a word to me as I bent over him and moisten-
ed his lips.

He told me while lying there the reason why he did
not stop sooner.   Something had got loose on the inside
throttle gearing, and he could not shut off steam, nor,
owing to some unaccountable complicity of evil, could he
reverse his engine.   So on he had to come, pell-mell,
and both of them were killed; for the fireman had jumped on some rocks, and must have died instantly, as he
was most horribly mangled.

The night wind moaned through the wreck, the drip-
ping water yet hissed upon the still hot iron of the engine, the waves of the river gurgled and rippled among
the rocks of the shore, and an occasional bellow of agony
was heard from amidst the cattle cars, where all the rest
of the hands were at work releasing the poor creatures;
but I sat there, in sad and solemn silence, waiting for him
to die that had been as a brother to me.   At last, just as

we heard the whistle of the approaching engine, and just as the rising sun had begun to gild and bespangle the purpling east, George opened his eyes, gave my hand a faint grasp, and was no more. I stood alone with the dead man I had loved so in life, but from whom death had now separated me.

14

AN UNROMANTIC HERO.

AN UNROMANTIC HERO.

THOSE who have traveled much on the Little Miami Railroad, must have noticed a little old fellow, with grizzled locks and an unpoetical stoop of the shoulders, who whisks about his engine with all the activity of a cat, and whom the railroad men all call "Uncle Jimmy." That is old Jimmy Wiggins, an engineer of long standing and well known. I believe Uncle Jimmy learned the machinists' trade with Eastwick & Harrison, in Philadelphia; at all events he has been railroading for a long time, and has been always noted for his carefulness and vigilance. Let me attempt to describe him. He is about five feet four inches in height, stoop-shouldered and short-legged. His hair is iron-gray, and his face would be called any thing but beautiful. He has, though, a clear blue eye that looks straight and firmly into yours with an honest and never-flinching expression, that at once convinces you that he is a " game " man.   Not very careful about his dress is old Jimmy ; grease spots abound on all his clothing, and his hands are usually begrimed with the marks of his trade. In short, Uncle Jimmy is any thing but a romantic-looking fellow, and a novelist would hesitate long before taking him as the hero of a romance ; but the old man is a hero, and under that rough, yet placid exterior, there beats a heart that never cools, and a will that never flinches.   We go back into the history of the past ages to find our heroes, and them we almost worship, but I question whether the whole history of the world furnishes a better example of self-sacrificing heroism, than this same rough and unromantic looking Jimmy Wiggins.   It is not the casket that gives value to the jewel ; it is the jewel gives value to all.   So with Uncle Jimmy ; rough he looks, but the heart he has makes him an honor to the race, and deserving of our praise.   I'll tell you now why I think so.

Uncle Jimmy was running a train that laid by on the switch at Spring Valley for the Up Express to pass.   He got there on time, and the express being a little behind time, the old man took advantage of the time to oil around.

The whistle of the up train was heard, but he paid no heed thereto, for it was to pass without stopping. The fellow who attended to the switch stood there at his post. Uncle Jimmy was coolly at work, when a shriek from the conductor called his attention, and looking up, he saw what would frighten and unnerve almost any one. The stupid fool at the switch had thrown it wide open, and the express was already on the branch, coming too at the rate of thirty miles an hour—thirty feet in the beat of your pulse—and his train loaded with passengers stood there stock-still. That was a time to try the stuff a man was made of; ordinary men would have shrunk from the task, and run from the scene. Your lily-handed, romantic gentry would have failed then, but homely old Jimmy Wiggins rose superior to the position, and, unromantic though he looks, proved a hero. No flinch in him. What though two hundred tons of matter was being hurled at him, fifty feet in the second? —what though the chances for death for him were a thousand to one for safety? No tremor in that brave old heart, no nerveless action in that strong arm. He leaped on to the engine, and with his charge met the shock; but his own engine was reversed, and under motion backwards when the other train struck it. It all took but an instant of time, but in that moment old Jimmy Wiggins concentrated more of true courage than many a man gets into in a lifetime of seventy years. The collision was frightful; iron and wood were twisted and jammed together as if they were rotten straw. Charley Hunt, the engineer of the other train, was instantly killed; passengers were wounded; terror, fright and pain held sway. Death was there, and all stood back appalled at what had occurred; yet all shuddered more to think of what would have been the result had Old Jimmy's engine stood still, and all felt a trembling anxiety for his fate, for surely, thought they, "in that wreck his life must have been the sacrifice to his bravery;" but out of the mass, as cool, as calm as when running on a straight track, crawled Uncle Jimmy, unhurt. He still runs on the same road, and long may his days be, and happy.

THE DUTIES OF AN ENGINEER.

THE DUTIES OF AN ENGINEER.

Those unacquainted with the duties of an engineer, are apt to think that they are extremely light, and require him simply to sit upon his seat and, shutting off or letting on the steam, regulate the speed of his engine. Although this is a part of the duty, still it is but a small portion, and for the benefit of those of my readers who are not posted on the matter, I will briefly state a few of the things he has to think of.

Say we take the engine lying in the shop cold, and an order comes for him to go out on the road. There is no water in the boiler; he must see that it is filled up to the proper level, and that the fire is started. He must know beforehand that no piece of the machinery is broken or loosened, so as to endanger the engine. To know this, he must make a personal inspection of every part of the engine—trucks, wheels, drivers, cranks, rods, valves, gearing, coupling, flues, scales, journals, driving-boxes, throttle gear, oil cups; in short, every thing about the engine must be seen to by him personally. He must know that every journal, every joint on the whole machine is in proper order to receive the oil necessary to lubricate it, for they will each and all receive a pretty severe strain in his coming ride, and, unless well oiled, will be pretty apt to get warm. He must know whether the flues are tight, or whether there are any leaks in the boiler to cause him trouble, or render it necessary for him to carry a light pressure of steam. He must see that there is water in the tank, and wood upon the tender; that he has upon the engine the tools usually necessary in case of a breakdown, such as hammers, chisels, wrenches, tongs, bolts, nuts, coupling-pins, plugs for the flues in case one should burst, chains, extra links, jack-screws, crow, and pinch-bars, an axe or hatchet; waste or rags, oil, tallow for the cylinders, and material for packing any joint that may give out. All this he must see to and know before he starts. And then, when steam is up, he can go. Now he must closely watch his time-card, and run so as to make the various stations on time. He must know that his watch is correct and in good order. He must see closely to his pumps that they work right, and that the water keeps at the proper level in the boiler. He must watch the scales that the pressure of the steam does not get too great, also the working of his engine. To the exhausts of the steam his ear must be as sensitive as a musical composer would be to a discord, for by it he can tell much of the condition of his engine, the set and play of the valves, and the condition of the many joints in the working machinery. At the same time he must keep the strictest watch of the track ahead of him, ready-nerved for any emergency that can possibly arise ; it may be a broken rail, cattle on the track, some stubborn, hasty fool striving to cross the track ahead of him, a broken bridge, washed out culvert, a train broken down ; or it may be some stranger frantically swinging his hands, and, in every manner possible, endeavoring to attract his attention. Something may happen to his train or his engine, and he must keep the strictest watch of both ; his hands must be ready to blow the whistle, shut off steam or reverse his engine, on the instant intimation of danger, for his engine gets over the ground at a rapid rate, and nothing but a cool nerve and stout arm can stop it, perhaps not these. And if any thing does happen rendering it necessary for him to stop, he cannot say to anybody, " Here, do this ; " he must go at it himself; and oftentimes, though it be but a trivial thing, it will tax his ingenuity to the utmost to repair it. Thus he goes on every day, be it clear or cloudy, whether summer breeze fill the air with balm, or the chill winds of winter make the road-bed solid as the rock, and the iron of the rails and wheels as brittle as glass ; whether the rain, pelting down, makes of every tiny brook a torrent or the drifted snow blockades the track, and his engine has to plunge into the chilly mass; through it all his eye must never cease its vigil, nor his arm lose its cunning. In cold weather he must watch the pumps that they do not freeze while standing at the stations, or the wheels get fractured by the frost; and, in cold or warm weather, he must keep watch of every place where there is the slightest friction, and keep it well oiled. At every station where time is allowed, he must give the whole engine a close inspection, lest some little part be out of order, and endangering some larger and more important piece of the machinery. At last, after this his journey for the day is ended, his work is by no means done. He must again inspect his engine, and

if there is any thing out of order, so much that he cannot without assistance repair it, he must apply at head-
quarters for the necessary aid. But there are a hundred
little matters that he can attend to himself; these he must
see to and do. The friction and enormous strain necessarily wears the brasses of the journals, and creates what
he calls " lost motion," that is, the journal moves in its
box loosely without causing the required motion in the part
of the machinery with which it is connected; this he must
remedy by various expedients. The spring-packing of the
piston may have worn loose, and require to be set out;
some one of the numerous steam joints may be leaking,
and these he must repack. Some of the flues may also be
leaking; if so, he must tighten them; or there may be a
crack in the boiler that leaks which can be remedied by
caulking; this he must do. The grate-bars may be broken
or disarranged; he must enter the fire-box and arrange
them. The packing in the pumps may have worn so as
to render their operation imperfect, or the valves may be
out of order, or the strainer between the tank and the
pump may be clogged; if either or all be the case, he must
take down the pump and rectify the matter. The smoke-
stack also may be clogged with cinders, or the netting

over it may be choked so as to impede the draught; if so, he must remedy it, or see that it is done. Some of the orifices through which oil is let on to the machinery may be clogged or too open; these he must see to. One or more of the journal-boxes of the wheels may need re-packing, and he must do it. An eccentric may have slipped a little, or a valve-rod been stripped, or a wheel be defective, or a tire on the driving-wheel may be loose, and have to be bolted on or reset. A gauge-cock may be clogged, a leaf of a spring broke, or the boiler may be very dirty and want washing out. Any of these things or a hundred others may have happened, and require his attention, which must on all occasions be given to it; for each part, however simple, goes to make up a whole, that, if out of repair, will render imminent a fearful loss of life and limb.

Thus the engineer rides every day, having the same care, and facing the same dangers, with the same responsibility resting on him. Who then shall say that, though he be grimy and greasy, rough and uncouth, given to tobacco-chewing, and sometimes to hard swearing, he is of no consequence to the world? Who shall blame him too severely if sometimes he makes an error?

www.ingramcontent.com/pod-product-compliance
Lightning Source LLC
Chambersburg PA
CBHW030116030726
47498CB00007B/2409